WOOING THE WICCAN

ELF MAGIC
BOOK 1

LOUISA MASTERS

Wooing the Wiccan

Copyright © 2025 by Louisa Masters

Cover Photo: Wander Aguiar

Model: Douglas

Cover Design: Booksmith Design

Editor: Hot Tree Editing

All rights reserved.

This is a work of fiction. Names, characters, places, events and incidents either are the product of the author's imagination or are used fictitiously, and any resemblance to persons, living or dead, business establishments, events or locales is entirely coincidental.

To the extent that the image or images on the cover of this book depict a person or persons, such person or persons are merely models and are not intended to portray any character or characters featured in the book.

WOOING THE WICCAN

I'm surrounded by two hundred thousand elves, yet somehow, I'm still lonely.

After a rough few millennia, the past decade has finally brought us peace and security—and justified my choices as our leader. But as chaos gives way to calm, I have more time for myself... yet it's not what I want it to be. I've been alone for a long time, but before my people and work needed me more. Now the lonely hours stretch into eternity.

Until I meet Jared.

He's my perfect match in every way; a teacher, a gardener, a cat dad. He loves books, nature, and interacting with others. He's sweet, funny, kind, and we're fire in the bedroom. The only hiccup? He's human, and he doesn't know other species exist.

Legally, we haven't been together long enough for me to tell him I'm not human, and it's getting harder and harder to keep this secret. To keep part of myself from him... to lie. But what if he learns the truth—a truth that will shatter the core of his beliefs—and can't handle it?

What if he can't forgive the lies?

CHAPTER ONE

Jared

"Bye, Mr. Veddy!" one of my tiny students lisps, grinning and waving at me as her grandmother ushers her out of my classroom. I wave back, my grin just as wide as hers despite the fact that I'm exhausted and desperate for coffee. The kids were super hyped up today, and I haven't had a second to think like an adult since I got here and found an impatient parent waiting at my classroom door, full of apologies about an early meeting he had to race off to, and I didn't mind if Josh hung out with me, did I?

I did, in fact, mind, since I have a long list of things to get done before my students arrive, but he was already halfway down the hall, and Josh was smiling hopefully. So I mentally waved goodbye to my quiet organization time and unlocked the classroom door.

Now, though... now I finally have a quiet moment. I close my eyes and inhale deeply, then exhale, releasing all the cares and stresses of the day on my breath. When I open my eyes again, I feel much more centered—and ready to take on the last jobs of the day before I can go home.

At this point in the school year, my students are pretty good at tidying up—well, as good as any five-year-old is. They know where everything belongs, and our end-of-day tidy-up is now part of their routine, so there are very few things still out of place. I'll grab those and put them away, then do my usual round with the disinfectant spray—little kids are adorable, but also gross.

I'm nearly finished when Gretchen, the other kindergarten teacher, wanders through the connecting door between our classrooms.

"Ready?" she asks, then does a double-take at the paintings drying on the line that bisects the room. "Jared, please tell me one of your kids didn't paint a giant c—" She cuts herself off, looks around to make sure there isn't a parent or child ready to surprise us at the worst possible moment, then leans forward to whisper, "Cock."

I laugh. "It looks like it, doesn't it? I was having visions of the very awkward parent meeting I'd have to call. But I've been reliably advised that it's one of those bladeless tower fans wearing a hat."

She squints and tilts her head to the left. "I... guess?"

"That's what innocent minds think, and I'm not going to question it. Ready for the staff meeting?"

"As much as I'll ever be. I'm nearly a hundred percent sure that I'm going to get voluntold to do something extra for the holiday concert."

I grab my jacket and satchel and follow her out into the hallway, pausing to turn off the lights and lock the door. "The holiday concert hasn't even been discussed yet. Wait until the usual tasks have been assigned before you worry about anything extra."

She tsks and shakes her head. "I don't know how you

get through life with that positive attitude, Jared. If you're not prepared for the worst, it blindsides you."

"If you spend your whole life worrying about things that haven't happened and might not, you take on a burden that isn't yours to carry," I counter. It took me a long time to accept that, and, being the imperfect human I am, sometimes it's still hard to live it. Carrying burdens that shouldn't have been mine to begin with was the norm in my family, and it wasn't until I was in my late twenties and had put some distance between myself and my upbringing that I realized how toxic it was for me.

Gretchen makes a sound that's part chuckle, part sigh. "I honestly don't know if you're naturally so chill or if becoming Wiccan did that for you. Sometimes I wish I'd known you before so I could compare."

I hold the door to the staffroom open for her, my other hand instinctively coming up to rest on where my amethyst pendant lies under my sweater. "It's a bit of both." Becoming a witch definitely taught me to let go of the things I couldn't control and embrace the parts of me I like best, but even as a kid, I was pretty laid-back.

She winks at me as we take our seats. "Whatever it is, it's working. You're awesome."

The principal stands and begins to speak before I can tell her she's awesome too. Another great life lesson: Hold on to the friends who raise you up, and let go of the ones who drag you down.

It's a little later than I'd planned when I get home, because Gretchen was totally right and the vice principal had already made a list of holiday concert tasks that she planned to pressure us into taking on in addition to what we already have to do for our classes. I'm now in charge of coordinating the final numbers we can expect on the night, which means my colleagues are going to quickly learn to hate me as I nag them to follow up parent RSVPs.

I drop my satchel by the front door, hang my coat on the peg I installed for it, and remove my shoes, setting them neatly on the rack. I like to leave my "outside things" in the little entryway, a line of demarcation between my time in the hectic world and the haven I've turned my home into. The scent of the incense I was burning last night lingers, mixing with the tang of the lemon oil I use in everything—soap, shampoo, moisturizer, room spray— and thanks to the app on my phone that controls my lamps, the living room is already lit with a cozy glow as I pad through the doorway in my socked feet.

"Pspsps." I continue toward the tiny kitchen, listening for the sound of Marge's almost-silent feet. She used to sneak up on me easily, but she's getting older now and doesn't play games as much.

She appears from behind the couch, stalking toward me with her tail in the air and head held high. It's her Queen of the House walk, and it usually means she thinks I haven't been giving her enough attention. I rectify that immediately, kneeling and giving her all the pets and scratches she demands, until she pulls away and heads for the kitchen, looking at me over her shoulder. The queen wants dinner.

I get her settled with her food dish and put one of the meal portions I prepped on the weekend in the oven to heat up for my own dinner before going to the bedroom to change into sweatpants and a hoodie. My cottage is a dream come true, but it's small, cold in winter and hot in summer, desperately needs to be updated, and isn't in the best neighborhood. There's a reason a kindergarten teacher was able to afford to buy a house in this economy —nobody else wanted it.

That's not entirely true—the older couple who lived here before they moved to an assisted living community had a few offers, but they liked me best, even though mine wasn't the highest. They insisted that if they had to leave their home, they wanted to know they were leaving it in good hands. It's one of the nicest compliments I've been paid, and I hope they're still happy with their choice. I know I am—for all its flaws, the house has amazing energy, and the small fenced yard out the back gives me ample space for a herb garden and outdoor rituals. The heating might not be great, but that just gives me an excuse to wrap myself in a blanket while I'm watching TV or reading. Marge and I are happy here, and I can make little improvements over time.

Back in the kitchen, I turn on my laptop and log in to my email while I'm waiting for dinner. This is the time of day when I browse social media and reply to personal emails. I used to have the apps on my phone, but when I found myself twitching toward it every time I heard a notification, I decided it was time to delete them. The kids deserve every ounce of my attention when I'm at school, and that applies to other tasks as well. If I want to check something from my phone, I can always log in via a browser, but having to actually take those steps usually stops me from doing it for anything nonessential.

I reply to a few messages on Facebook and Instagram and comment on a post I've been tagged in, then switch to my email. I can scroll while I eat, but I've learned the hard way not to try typing and eating at the same time.

First is an email from an old coworker who moved to Canada, asking if we can catch up when she comes home for the holidays. That's a lovely surprise, and I immediately reply in the affirmative. Next is a newsletter from the travel agent I used last time I went on vacation, a sales email from a clothing store, a quick note from a college friend confirming our next dinner, what looks like spam, another sales—

My eyes slide back up to the email I thought was spam, and I read the subject line again. *Deepen Your Ability to Use Magic.* I'm not sure what's caught my attention—it still looks like spam to me. I get emails like this sometimes, probably because I occasionally buy supplies online. Usually I prefer to visit local stores, and living in a densely populated area means I have options to choose from, but there have been times when a particular bowl or something that I see online calls to me. One of the stores must have sold their mailing list, though, because I don't know why else I'd be getting emails from random senders that are targeted to my interests. Magic is something the scammers frequently use to tempt me into opening and clicking... not that I'd ever click something in an unsolicited email from a stranger.

My finger hovers over the Delete key, but instinct niggles, and instead, I click to open the email.

To my surprise, it's addressed to me personally. I don't usually put my actual name when I shop online, preferring to use initials instead, but this email begins with *Dear Jared.* The next line mentions getting my contact information from a friend of mine, another witch, and I reach for my phone and call her.

"...set the damn table before I throw the Xbox in the trash! Hi, Jared. It's been a while."

I'm sure she can hear my smile when I say, "Hey, Mel. Yeah, that's my fault. I never rescheduled after I had to cancel that time. Listen, I'm sorry to bother you at dinner-time—I can tell you're busy—"

"Hah! Try and find a time that isn't busy around here, I dare you."

"I've known you long enough to know that's impossible. I won't keep you—though I will text you later to set up lunch or something. But I got this email that says you gave them my c—"

"Crap! I totally spaced, didn't I? I was supposed to let you know I'd passed along your email, and I didn't. I'm so sorry."

Wow. Okay, then. "So it's legit? This email about learning to use magic?"

She must hear my skepticism, because she snorts. "I know, right? The first time I got called about it, I hung up. There are so many people who think we'll fall for any scam just because we're Wiccan, like that makes us gullible. But I eventually went to one of their seminars, and now I go to weekly classes. It's legit, and I think you'd get a lot out of it. It's free, anyway, so you might as well check it out."

"Free?" That can't be right.

"Volunteer run," she confirms. "It's genuinely for those of us who want to be more connected to nature, and the benefits I'm seeing after only a couple of months are wonderful. I— For the love of the goddess, Mikey, stop throwing stuff at your sister! I don't care what she said, we don't throw things at people! Jared, listen, I've gotta go. Talk later?"

"Yeah, sure," I reply, but she's already ended the call.

I put my phone down and read the email properly. There's not a lot of detail there—basically what Mel just told me, plus dates, times, and locations for information sessions where I can learn more. There is some emphasis on this being for further learning only, with no products or services to buy.

"What do you think, Margie?" I ask. "It looks sus, but Mel wouldn't scam me... and my gut says it's worth checking out."

My cat looks up from her food bowl and meows disinterestedly. Guess the decision's up to me, then.

CHAPTER TWO

Raðulfr

"SAY BYE, CECY," Percy coaxes, his daughter perched comfortably on his hip while he sets an example by waving at me. Cecylia obediently waves.

"Bye-bye!" Then her eyes go wide as she realizes what that means, and her little face crumples. "Nooooooo. Stay here!"

Aww. "I wish I could, Cecy, but I have to go home now." I probably shouldn't have come in the first place, given the amount of work I brought home with me this weekend, but it's hard to resist a visit to Here Be Dragons. It's so comfortable and welcoming here... though not really restful. Dragons never are.

But restful or not, I'm never lonely when I'm here, and unfortunately, loneliness has become too big a part of my life to pretend that doesn't matter. It's ridiculous—I'm responsible for nearly two hundred thousand elves, for their safety and wellbeing and happiness, and I'm welcomed enthusiastically by them wherever I go, yet somehow, I'm still lonely.

Cecy sticks out her bottom lip in a stubborn pout. "Stay." She pats my chest. "Dis new home."

I chuckle, and Percy outright laughs. "How am I supposed to resist that?" I ask him, and, sensing weakness, Cecy reaches for me.

I step back, putting my hands behind me. That sweet little dragonet inherited a natural streak of manipulation ability, and learned to hone it from Brandt and Dustin. If I hold her, I'll be a goner.

Her eyes fill with tears. "Rosh," she whines piteously. It's the closest she can get to pronouncing my name, and I never thought the sound would be so dear to me. "Stay, Rosh." Her mouth trembles, and I waver.

"Oh, sweet one, I wish I could." Maybe if I move—

"Don't let her guilt you, Raðulfr," Percy warns. "You spent two hours playing blocks with her. It's time for her nap, anyway."

That's clearly some kind of reverse magic word, because Cecy hisses and immediately shifts into her dragon form. Percy adjusts his hold on her without batting an eye—a far cry from the first time she did it.

"You still have to nap," he tells her. She's no longer baby pale, her coloring beginning to darken from almost white to the blue she'll be as an adult. Brandt was sighing about that the other day.

"I'm going to leave you to fight this battle," I say as Cecy gives a tiny growl. Percy taps her on the nose.

"None of that. We don't growl at family just because we don't like naps," he chides, then turns his attention back to me. "I sometimes can't tell if I win this battle or not. Safe travels home, and come see us again soon. Cecy misses her Uncle Rosh." His gentle smile is genuine, and not for the first time, I envy Brandt. Not because of Percy, specifically, though Percy is wonderful, but because he has a loving, supportive partner and a family. I lost the only family I had long ago, and it hurt, but there were thousands of others who needed me.

Now that we're not on the brink of extinction—that they know of—they don't need me quite so much.

I give Percy and Cecy another little wave and leave them in the sunroom at the back of the house, making my way to the kitchen, where my bodyguard for the day is sitting at the table, enjoying a cup of something—tea, probably, if I know the dragons—and gossip. Dragons always have good gossip, probably because they create so much of it.

Niamh looks up when I enter and smiles. "Ready to go, sir?"

"Only when you are. Don't abandon your drink before it's finished."

Kethe, who's been looking after Brandt's household for more years than I can remember—possibly more than I've been alive—chuckles fondly. "You've always been considerate." She's sitting opposite Niamh and reaches out to nudge a plate of cookies in my direction. "Have some."

I take one—I'm not stupid, and Kethe's one of the best cooks I've ever met, in this dimension or the one we came from.

"I'm ready, Your Majesty," Niamh assures me, standing. "This is my third cuppa. The others will be so jealous they weren't on duty today."

I don't say anything, but I'm grinning on the inside. I'm well aware that being on duty when I come to visit Here Be Dragons is a perk for my security staff. This is very likely the safest place in existence, thanks to Steffen, Brandt's head of security and resident paranoid conspiracy theorist. There's really no reason for me to need security here, except that it's customary for me to go nowhere unguarded. So whoever has bodyguard duty when I'm here gets to sit down with a snack and good company, relieved of any concern for my safety beyond Cecy accidentally scratching me with her needle-sharp little dragon claws. There are worse things.

We say our goodbyes to Kethe, and then Niamh opens a portal back to my two-story penthouse condo with the incredible roof garden that sometimes allows me to almost forget I'm in the middle of the city. She does her usual check that nobody's broken in, then asks if I need anything. I don't, of course, and she heads into the butler's suite—because yes, this condo has a butler's suite. It was one of the reasons my security team liked it so much. The room with an en suite bathroom and tiny kitchenette gives my bodyguard of the day some privacy and prevents me from feeling like I'm being watched all the time.

There are moments when I'm tempted to knock on the door and ask my guard to come and talk to me, but so far, I've resisted. As nice as they all are, and as much as we get along, in the end, they'd still be talking to me because it's their job. It doesn't have quite the same effect when I think of it that way.

I wander through the quiet rooms, up the stairs to the den and through the french windows into the garden. It really is an excellent garden, and I spend most of my time at home out here. I'm not made for city living. Even back on our homeworld, I chafed at the need to be in cities most of the time.

And then the anomalies began, and the cities slowly disappeared. Along with everything else.

Shaking off the gloomy thoughts, I sink to my knees in

the soft grass beside a lemon tree. I'm not sure why, but I have a strong connection with lemon trees. The scent, maybe? Even when the fruit isn't going, the leaves have such a fresh fragrance.

From far below, the faint hum of traffic flavors the air, and the scent of my lemon tree surrounds me. This isn't so bad. I have a good life here, and I kept more of my people alive than I thought would be possible. Fifteen years ago, I was sure we'd all be dead by now. We're not, and that's a miracle.

The life force surrounds me, as if it knows I'm trying to cheer myself up, and for just a second, I forget how lonely I am.

"THERE'S JUST ONE MORE THING," Caolan says, tapping the screen of his tablet. "We've had a request for you to attend a sporting event."

I blink at him. "What?" Nobody told me our weekly briefing was going to include sports today.

He shrugs. "I don't have much information. The PR team asked me to mention this to you. Apparently an elf has joined the management of a local team, and I guess they want to get more elves involved and think your patronage will help."

That's not unreasonable. "What's the sport?"

Caolan shrugs. "No idea. I can ask PR to put together a briefing."

"That's probably the best path to take for now. Unless there's a reason you can think of for me to outright refuse?"

Eoin, my head of security, makes a note. "Let me talk

to PR directly and check whether we'd be able to make security arrangements. If that checks out, there's no problem from my side."

"Nor mine," Caolan adds. "It might be good for you. In fact—"

The knock on the door thankfully interrupts what I know was going to be a well-meaning lecture about needing to take more time for leisure. "Enter," I call. We're nearly done with this meeting anyway.

The door opens, and the woman who slips inside is one I've known for a long time. If you need a problem solved, Caoimhe is the one to turn to. Without her, it's entirely likely we wouldn't have survived long enough to migrate to Earth. Now, she's our liaison on the team working to restore balance to the life force here. It's a complicated project in which humans are being taught to use and embrace their innate magic skills *without* also learning that they're not the only higher-intelligence species on this planet. If she and the others fail, we'll all slowly lose our abilities and the heritage of our species. I don't envy her this task.

"Sorry to interrupt, Your Majesty," she says. "I wondered if Caolan or Eoin was free for an hour at five?"

Caolan makes a face even as Eoin shakes his head. "Sorry, Caoimhe, we have a meeting with the combined security team at two that's likely to last into the evening. It's quarterly review time."

I don't envy them *that* task, either—Steffen Draco, Brandt's head of security, is... exacting.

"Damn. It was a long shot, but I was hoping... Oh well."

"What's the problem?" I ask.

She shakes her head. "It's not a disaster. Pete, the

human who's been teaching some of our classes, has this month off because his wife just had their first child. She's the cutest little thing—did you know baby vampires are born with fangs? They're retracted and don't descend until they're older, but you can see the little teeth through their gums."

"Aww," Caolan says, and we all smile at each other, possibly looking foolish, but tiny babies who belong to other people are worth cooing over.

"Anyway," Caoimhe says, "we've been covering his classes, but someone called in sick today, and I can't find anyone who can help. It has to be a magic-capable human, sorcerer, elf, or dragon—someone who can see at least some of what's being done and step in to avert any disasters."

"Hmm," Caolan muses. "Maybe one of us could slip out of the meeting to take the class?"

Eoin looks at him incredulously. "Do you want to be the one to tell Steffen that there's an unexpected situation where someone called in sick and now one of us needs to supervise humans using magic?"

Caoimhe grimaces. "Please don't. I don't have time to deal with an interrogation today."

"I can do it." I hear the words, but it takes me a moment to realize that I said them. I was *thinking* it was something I could probably handle, but I didn't exactly plan to volunteer.

The three surprised faces I get are a little annoying, though.

"You can, sir?" Caoimhe asks, then coughs. "I mean, we couldn't possibly bother you with this. I'll just send the students a message that today's class is cancelled."

My hackles rise. "You'll do no such thing. I've been

spellcasting for a long time, I'm free at five, and I'm perfectly capable of intervening if it seems like a human is going to set something on fire. Do I need to teach them anything in particular?" Human magic is slightly different from ours, so I'm not sure how effective I'd be at that.

She slowly shakes her head. "No-o... this group has been learning for a while, and mostly Pete just supervises them and encourages them to try something new. Noah put together a list of things they can experiment with that aren't dangerous, and once each class masters the basic skills, they work through those." She hesitates. "Are you sure...?"

"Absolutely," I declare. "After all, it will affect me just as much as anyone if humans fail to use magic. Leave it with me." If nothing else, it's another hour where I can feel a little less lonely.

CHAPTER THREE

Jared

IF SOMEBODY HAD ASKED me last year—just two months ago—if I'd be attending regular workshops on using magic, I would have laughed hard enough to end up with a pinched nerve (that's actually something that happens when you're in your forties, as I discovered the hard way). After all, magic is personal. It's ritual, a communication with nature and the god and goddess. It's not something you can learn in a classroom.

Yet here I am, fully willing to admit how wrong I was. I might have been skeptical at that first session, but I can't deny that the last couple of months have put me closer in contact with my own spirituality and the essence of the world than I've ever been. Pete, our guide—it seems foolish to call him a teacher when he insisted from the beginning that he's just here to give us more confidence as we learn—has been very open about using magic to feel more connected to the world and wanting to help others do the same. During the information session, he spoke in detail about how, while our inner magic can't be used to actively harm, it can be manipulated to do so indirectly.

He didn't outright say it, but I inferred that was why he and his fellow volunteers only contact people who've been personally referred to them, rather than advertising on a wider scale. Do no harm is one of the edicts I live my life by, but not everyone in the world feels the same, and given what I've learned to use magic to do, I can see how it would be easy for someone to weaponize it. I use magic fire to light candles, but someone else might use it to start a forest fire—or set a building alight.

I stroll into the room at the community center where our weekly sessions are held and glance toward the front to say hi to whoever's filling in for Pete tonight. They've all been great, and I'm glad Pete's spending time with his newborn, but I'll be...

...

...huh.

I trip over my own feet and grab the nearest table to save myself from ending up on the floor.

"Whoa! You okay, Jared?" Lynn, one of the other attendees, asks, and heat floods my cheeks.

"Yes, fine. I'm so sorry. I put my foot down wrong." It's partly true, but I'm not going to say the rest out loud. I'm embarrassed enough without adding, *"Because I want to lick that man all over. Our teacher for today? He can teach me anything he wants."* No. Nope.

But damn, I'd forgotten how long it's been since I had sex, and one look at the man leaning against the table up the front has brought all my needs and urges to the fore.

Gathering what's left of my pride, I slide into my usual seat before looking back toward the man who's definitely going to be the star of all my future fantasies. "Hi. I'm Jared."

His mouth is curved into a smile, but somehow I know

he's not laughing at me. Taking a moment to actually absorb the details of his face, I concede that he's never going to get work as a model. He's not classically attractive —his lips are too thin, his nose a little larger than what most consider aesthetically pleasing. His hair is dark blond and long enough to be pulled into a braid that's hanging over one shoulder. The neat, silky-looking beard that hugs his jaw is a shade darker, and his eyes are a warm gray. He seems older than he looks, though I can't say why. Overall, I'm not sure what it is about him that makes me want to beg him to take me home and keep me, but my instincts are only saying good things about him.

"It's nice to meet you, Jared," he says, and of course he has to have a nice voice too, and a sexy accent, because the goddess didn't already bless him with enough. "I'm Raðulfr."

Welp, I found a problem with my plan for us to spend eternity together. I can't pronounce his name.

I sometimes run into this issue with my students, but usually I have the class list ahead of time and can google how to pronounce unfamiliar names, so that on the first day, I at least have a shot at getting it close. That's not an option here—my ears heard what he said, but my brain doesn't know how to process it.

"I'm so sorry, I'm not familiar with that name and I really want to get it right. Could you say it again, more slowly?"

His smile doesn't change, and I hope that means I haven't offended him. "Of course. Thank you for asking. It's Raðulfr." He slows it down, but I still don't quite catch it, and I'm wondering if I dare ask again when he breaks it into syllables, "Roh-low-lish."

Ohhh. I can say that. I repeat it, but somehow it

sounds different. Maybe it's the accent? He doesn't seem upset, though.

"Excellent."

"It's not quite right," I apologize, and his smile widens.

"You're close, and you're trying. I appreciate that effort."

God and goddess, could he be more perfect? I open my mouth, probably to ask if he wants me to be his sex toy, but thankfully I'm interrupted when three more people enter.

Raðulfr lingers for a moment, then turns to greet them, and I exhale deeply.

"Wow," Lynn murmurs beside me.

"I know."

"Thanks for asking about the name, by the way. I was definitely not going to get it right. I still might not."

I make an agreeing noise, and she leans closer.

"He has the most beautiful aura of anyone I've ever seen. Do you see it?" she whispers.

I can't see auras the way she can, but I know exactly what she means. "Yeah. There's something about him." And I don't just mean whatever it is that's causing my sexual attraction to him.

Finally, everyone's arrived and settled, and Raðulfr straightens and bestows that gorgeous smile on us all. "I think you've all heard me introduce myself already, but in case you didn't, my name is Raðulfr and I'm filling in for Pete tonight. I haven't met his daughter myself, but I've been told she's the sweetest baby and that Pete is completely in love with her—just as he should be."

There are a few awws, and I wonder if, when Pete comes back, we can talk him into bringing his daughter to meet us. I adore kids of all ages, but there's something special about the tiny ones.

"I'm given to understand that you've all been working independently, but if there's anything I can help with or if you have any questions, just let me know."

Henry, a young witch who grew up in a Wiccan family, half raises his hand. "I want to try gathering moisture for the first time. Could you watch me? I'd feel more confident that way."

Lynn elbows me, muffling a snicker. Henry's never lacked confidence in his life that I can tell—but he has flirted with every man to walk into this room. I try not to glare at the back of his head. It's not his fault he's attracted to Raðulfr.

We all break off to do our own thing, some people pairing up. I've done that a few times—it's interesting to see the way our magic can work in tandem or play off each other—but tonight I'm concentrating on mastering a new skill.

I'm pretty good at moving small objects and creating fire, and I've managed to gather moisture from the air a few times, though it's something I definitely need to practice. Next on my list, however, is manipulating air. We were all kind of surprised by how far down it was on the list we were given, but Pete just laughed and invited us to try it.

We failed. All of us. Air is barely tangible, and it's not easy to work with something you can't get hold of. Pete suggested we master some of the other magics first, to give ourselves experience with using it before tackling air. He was right—creating fire was exhausting the first time I did it, but now it's as easy as a thought. I can even juggle tiny fireballs, though I've only done it in class to practice. It's not practical or necessary in the real world.

So now that I have a better grasp on how to use magic and how *I* use magic—because apparently it's slightly different for everyone—I want to push myself to achieve more.

I close my eyes and take a deep, cleansing breath, then another, allowing the movement of the breath through my body to center me. From the moment Pete said meditation was a key part of learning magic, I knew I could trust what he was telling us. Magic is part of our connection with the world, part of the gift we're given by the god and goddess. Of course our ability to use it needs to come from deep inside us.

It only takes a moment for me to feel the rush of energy throughout my body—my inner life force, carried to every part of me by my blood. I widen my sensory awareness and feel the way the energy in me ebbs and flows with the energy of nature, surrounding me. The life force of the world, so to speak—though I'd never say that out loud. Next, I visualize what I want to do—air isn't exactly visible, so it's probably easiest if I try to use my other senses. A tickle of breeze on the back of my hand, perhaps. I think about how that would feel, cementing the concept of it in my mind. I'll even leave my eyes closed, so I'm not tempted to rely on them and potentially miss other sensory input.

The final step is the spell. For small magics and ones I'm very familiar with, I don't always use a spoken spell, but with something new or big or important, it's helpful and respectful to use words to shape and focus my intent. Barely moving my lips, I whisper,

"Breath of life, breath sublime,

Stir the air, dance softly.
A gentle touch, a tiny eddy,
Breath of life, move for me."

I'll never make it as a poet, but the words themselves don't necessarily matter—it's the intent that speaking a spell creates.

But my intent clearly needs more direction, because the air doesn't respond.

Shaking off my disappointment, I open my eyes. It's fine. I knew this was going to take me a while to get the hang of. I'll give myself a moment and then try again.

And again.

And again.

On my fifth attempt, it's harder to let go of my frustration. I should be feeling *something* by now, the tiniest touch of air.

"Hello again."

I look up into solemn gray eyes and wish the spell had worked so I could have shown off for Raðulfr. It's childish and ridiculous, but I wish it all the same.

"Hi. Uh, are you having a good time?" Mentally, I kick myself. At least Lynn's too busy with her spell to laugh at me right now.

Raðulfr nods. "I am, actually. It's delightful to see you all discovering this part of yourselves."

That gives me a warm little feeling. "How was it for you?" I ask impulsively. "When you first learned."

He makes a humming sound and slides into the chair beside me. "I can barely remember; it was so long ago. I felt... It was like all my life I'd been hearing music from afar. It was muffled, unclear, but still beautiful. And then as I learned spellcraft, the music became clearer and clearer, until I was standing in the midst of the most amazing symphony." He grimaces. "The actual learning part was frustrating. It still is—whenever I try a new spell, I feel as though a door slams closed between me and the music, and I have to work to get it open all over again. It's worth it, though."

"It is," I agree, though my smile is rueful. "That's a great analogy. I like it a lot more than mine, which is that I'm shackled and can't use magic until I get myself free."

A tiny frown flickers over his face. "Do you feel shackled by your life?" he asks quietly, surprising me.

"No. I mean... not really. No."

He watches me steadily and says nothing. I blow out a breath. "Not shackled, exactly. I have a good life that I love. There are some things that are still out of reach, but hey, that's normal, right?" I chuckle, but even to me it sounds forced. Definitely not putting my best foot forward tonight.

CHAPTER FOUR

Raðulfr

JARED'S FACE wears a clearly uncomfortable expression, but I can't let go of this subject yet. Perhaps I should—definitely, I should—but it's been a long time since I met someone who so instantly fascinated me in this way. There's physical attraction, yes, but that's easy enough to disregard. It was the way he so genuinely tried to learn my name that captured my attention. People who show true respect for others in that way are far rarer than they should be.

Truthfully, though, his looks do have something to do with it. His narrow features are interesting, but it's the warmth in his brown eyes and the wild way his dark curls tumble over his forehead that appeal to me the most. He's handsome in an approachable way.

I've been watching him for the past half hour. Even when I was helping others, part of my attention was on him. There are differences between the way humans use the life force and elf spellcasting, but we share enough similarities that I can see what he's trying to do. He has a lot of "magical" strength, and it's easy to tell that he's been diligent about practicing and building his ability. So far, these are all things I can respect deeply, and they just add to the interest I feel.

"It's in the nature of beings such as us to constantly be setting new goals and dreams for ourselves, especially when we attain the old ones. There will always be something that seems out of reach—and perhaps it is. Perhaps it will stay that way. The important part is how you cope with the knowledge that you may never reach it." I stop abruptly. I'm so used to giving counsel to my people that I'd forgotten for a moment that Jared isn't one of them. To him, I'm not the life force's representative to our species—I'm just a man he barely knows who's presuming to give him advice he never asked for. How embarrassing.

I sneak a glance toward the corner where Ari, my guard today, is standing behind some clever spellwork that hides his presence. Sure enough, he's watching with a big grin. This is definitely going to be discussed during the daily security briefing.

Holding in a sigh, I turn my attention back to Jared and say, "I'm sorry. I didn't mean to lecture. Force of habit."

To my surprise—and pleasure—he chuckles. "Please don't apologize. You're right. There are some things I may not ever get, and I still haven't processed that. I guess that contributes to the whole shackled thing."

Emotional maturity is so refreshing. I try to guess his age, but that's something I struggle with when it comes to humans. He's not old, but perhaps settled enough into life to understand himself.

"Do you think that's what's stopping me from manipulating air?" he asks, and I blink in surprise.

"No. You almost have it, in fact—a few more attempts should see success. Do you want to try again?"

Squaring his shoulders, he inhales deeply and nods. "Yes. Would you watch? Let me know if I'm getting off track?"

From what I've seen so far, he just needs to persevere, but I'm reluctant to give up the extra few moments with him, even if he will be concentrating on something else. "Of course."

He smiles at me and then closes his eyes. I see the way the life force moves around him as he draws it to him in preparation for shaping it to his purpose. His lips move, and though I'm sure he never intended for me to hear, elf hearing is better than human. Not as good as shifter, or even vampire, but still good enough for me to catch the words of his spell. The life force reacts to his intent, a little more strongly than before, but not enough.

Jared opens his eyes, his mouth twisting into a disappointed smile. "I'll keep trying."

"You're so very close," I assure him. "May I make a suggestion?"

He nods. "Please do."

"Instead of trying to create an air movement from scratch, try working with an existing movement. Just the first time, so you can get a sense of how it should feel."

A tiny line appears between his brows. "Do you mean try to capture the wind?"

"Oh, no!" Alarm floods me. "That would be ambitious. Leave the wind be for the time being. No, I meant..." I reach out and grab one of the small candles I put on each table before the class began, for anyone who wanted to practice with fire to use. There are also tiny paper espresso cups, for gathering water into. Beginners' tools that

Caoimhe gave me to bring. With barely a thought, I set it alight.

"Wow," Jared says. "You make it look so easy... but also a little different?" That line deepens.

"I've been doing this a long time," I say vaguely. I can't exactly tell this unknowing human that it looks different because I'm an elf. Time to distract. "So, when I hold the candle here"—I extend it to arm's length in front of me—"and blow with this amount of force"—I demonstrate with what is essentially a light exhale—"the movement of air isn't strong enough to reach and extinguish the candle. However, if I repeat it, and this time give it a little boost with a spell..." I exhale again, giving the air a tiny nudge with the life force, and the breath is augmented, extinguishing the candle and drifting over the skin of my hand. "It's sometimes easier to work with what already exists than to create something new."

There's a hint of excitement on his face now, and it makes me smile. "I never thought of that," he admits. "May I?" He holds out his hand for the candle, and I pass it to him. "You really must have been doing this for a long time," he says as he carefully lights it. He's very good with that small magic, not needing a spell or even to stop speaking as he does it. "You were very smooth when you put the candle out. I barely saw what you did, and I was watching for it."

Part of that was because he was watching for me to do it the way a human would. "Since I was a child," I say, again trying to distract him. I need to be more careful. "In my family, we're taught small spells as soon as we're old enough to understand how they work and the impact they have." That's completely true—all elves learn minor spell-casting at the same time we learn to read and write. It's an intrinsic part of our natures and lives. It used to be the same for humans—I remember clearly how in tune they were with their magic, before the species wars here on Earth changed the way the community existed. It deeply saddened me when we migrated here over a decade ago and I learned that humans had truly lost their ability to use magic. Until then, I'd hoped that the reports from my scouts were the result of incomplete information. Though the reasons for it are awful, it does give me a small measure of pleasure to know that some humans are relearning it.

No species should lose part of itself.

Jared holds the candle at arm's length. His hands are large, and his long fingers have some small smudges on them... paint? Is he an artist?

He blows gently, just as I did the first time, but doesn't reach for the life force. A practice run. I keep my expression neutral but inwardly applaud. This will give him a better idea of how the breath should feel and how much energy he needs to use.

On his second exhale, he draws power, whispering his spell. The flame flickers but doesn't quite go out. His delighted laugh puts to rest my concern that he would be disappointed.

"Did you see that? I *felt* it! It wasn't strong enough to put out the candle, but it was a lot stronger than naturally!" He grins at me. "I bet I get it next time."

I grin back and raise a brow. "I bet you do. Care to show me?"

He turns his gaze back to the candle, laughter fading into determination. Inhale, power, then—

"Yes!" The hand not holding the now-extinguished candle punches the air. "Wow, that feels good."

"Congratulations. That was very nicely done."

Jared lays the candle on the table and turns his happy face to me. "Thanks mostly to your excellent advice. Can I buy you a thank-you drink after this?"

Shocked, I hesitate. I can't remember the last time someone I just met wanted to engage with me socially. But then, most of them meet King Raðulfr, the species leader of the elves, and even if they might have wanted to, they assume I'm too busy or would say no.

I'm silent too long, because Jared's excitement dims to politeness. "Please don't feel obliged. It was just a thought, and I promise there are no hard feelings if you'd—"

"Yes," I blurt, and over in the corner, Ari straightens. If he was hoping for an early night, he'll be disappointed. "I'd like that."

Now it's Jared's turn to hesitate. "Are you sure? Because—"

"I'm very sure," I say firmly. "I was just surprised, but I'd enjoy that a lot. You don't have to buy my drink, though."

His smile reappears, and he shakes his head. "Yes, I do. But actually, is it okay if it's just coffee? I have work tomorrow, and I don't ever drink on a work night."

Excellent. That will save me from having to pretend to be affected by the alcoholic content of my drink. "Coffee would be perfect. Or dare I say, tea?"

"We are so destined to be friends," he jokes, and then his gaze goes over my shoulder. "I think you're needed, but I'll wait for you when we're done here and we can head out. There's a great indie bookstore two blocks from here that stays open late for college students, and it has a café."

"Perfect. Now... try moving the air from scratch." I wiggle my brows at him, immediately feeling foolish, but his chuckle as I stand and walk toward the woman who needs my help makes a little foolishness worthwhile.

It's not long after that when the class wraps up for the evening. As people begin to wander out, Jared starts in my direction, only to stop when a strident ringtone cuts through the air. He pulls a phone from his pocket and glances at the screen, then meets my gaze and points to the hall. I nod. I need to gather all the candles and cups and put the furniture back the way the community center requested.

As soon as the room is empty, Ari drops the spell that's been hiding him. "Sir, I say this in the most respectful way possible: *What* are you doing?"

"Tidying up," I reply calmly, my hands full of small tapers. "Could you grab the bag these were in?"

He obeys, but if I thought he'd let it go, I was so very wrong. "We don't have a security protocol in place for this."

"I've had tea in a public place before, Ari. We don't need a security protocol." I drop the candles in the bag and go back for the cups while he begins stacking chairs.

"Not with a stranger. A *human* stranger," he hisses.

"That makes it even safer. He has no idea who I am, and nor will anyone else at this bookstore, most likely. Not that there's any active threat to my safety anyway. You're beginning to sound like Steffen Draco." It gives me plenty of satisfaction to get that dig in.

Ari narrows his eyes. "If this is the kind of escapade Brandt gets up to, I'm beginning to understand why Steffen is so strict."

I laugh. "Escapade? It's a cup of tea in a bookstore café, to which I'm certain you'll follow us. That hardly counts as an escapade."

We move to rearrange the tables, and he says, "It does for you. Especially since you're doing it with an unknown human—and one who's seen you spellcast. Have you forgotten how big a danger humans present to the community?"

I pull out my trump card. "Not this one, or he wouldn't be here. Have you forgotten that Steffen insisted on a rigorous background check on every human invited to the program?"

He falls silent, and I savor the victory for a few seconds before relenting. "It's a cup of tea in a quiet café," I reiterate. "He has to work tomorrow, so we'll probably be all done and on our way home in an hour. He's been vetted, you'll be watching the whole time, and I promise to be careful and not give anything away. I work hard, Ari. Let me have this one small thing."

He sighs, and I know I've won.

CHAPTER FIVE

Jared

I HOVER IN THE HALLWAY, wondering what's come over me. I've never asked Pete or any of the others who've filled in for him to have a drink with me, and it can be argued that they all helped me more than Raðulfr—though his tip tonight about starting with something that already exists is a good one. I can already think of other things it will make so much easier.

But that's not the only reason I suggested this outing. It's not even the main one. I can't *actually* call this a date, because I've told Raðulfr it's just a thank-you drink, but I'm kind of maybe hoping that it will lead to one. Which is nerve-racking. It's been a good long while since I dated anyone, and longer still since it was someone I just met randomly. Usually I end up dating friends of friends or people I meet at teacher conferences or witchy events.

I guess a class on using magic counts as a witchy event. And it's a definite bonus that Raðulfr already knows I'm a witch and isn't bothered by it. A lot of people back off fast when they find out I'm Wiccan. Of course, the downside is that he doesn't know I'm interested in him that way.

Maybe he usually has a cup of tea at this time and figures I might as well pay for it. Maybe he's not interested in men. Maybe he's married or in a serious relationship. Maybe he felt bad saying no when I asked.

Maybe I need to stop overthinking this. It's a casual drink in a public place with an interesting man. That's all. Then I'll go home, get some sleep, and wake up to another day of teaching five-year-olds that "fingerpainting" doesn't mean "put paint on your mouth and nose and press your face to the paper." My life might not be thrilling, but it's mine and I like—

I frown. Is Raðulfr talking to himself? I'd swear I hear voices from inside the meeting room. Should I check on him?

I'm still trying to decide—and really, does it matter if he talks to himself? I talk to my cat—when the door opens and he comes out. As soon as he sees me, his face lights with a smile, and I let go of the foolish worries. It doesn't seem likely that he only agreed to come because he felt sorry for me, not if he's smiling like that.

"Ready?" he asks, and I nod.

"Is there anything you need to do here before we go? Check in with someone or...?" I have no idea how hiring a room in a community center works.

"No, it's all sorted. I just need to make sure this is closed." He pulls the door shut, then dusts off his hands. "Shall we?"

The night outside is crisp and cold, though warmer than it was just a few weeks ago. It's not quite spring, but on a night like tonight, I can begin to hope winter will soon be behind us. Not that I dislike winter—it has its good points—but I'm looking forward to getting out in my garden again.

"You're deep in thought," Raðulfr ventures as we stroll along the sidewalk. "Thinking about that spell?"

I mentally kick myself for wasting this opportunity. He's hardly going to want to get to know me better if I'm a silent lump. "No, actually. I was thinking of all the things I'd like to do in my garden come spring."

"You like to garden?" His delight warms me from top to toe. "So do I. Not that I get much chance these days, but I do have a small patch to potter in."

"Same," I confess. "Mostly I grow herbs and other bits and pieces I can use in practice, but I do like to add the occasional frivolous flower or tree." I snort. "A few years back, I bought a dwarf kumquat tree."

"Oh?" He tilts his head in curiosity. "I'm not familiar with... what did you call it? Komquill?"

"Kumquat," I repeat, grinning. "It's a fruit tree that's native to China. I bought it on a whim because it's pretty, but I wasn't prepared for the fruit."

"You can't finish the story like that," he protests. "Is the fruit bad?"

I shake my head. "No, but it didn't taste like I thought it would. When you first bite in, it's sweet, but the sour takes over very quickly. I like it for preserves and in cooking, but not so much for eating."

He chuckles. "Good thing you only got a dwarf tree then. Imagine if you had a full-size one full of fruit."

"There aren't enough jam jars in the world," I agree, slowing as we reach the bookstore. "Here we are." The plate-glass window glows with warm light from within, and I take a moment to glance at the current display. There's something so wonderful and welcoming about a bookstore.

Inside, Raðulfr glances around and then inhales deeply. "Ah. Books."

A young couple passing us on their way out snicker, and his cheeks tinge pink. It's adorable.

"It's a comforting smell, isn't it?" I ask. "It's silly in this age of technology, but I still find it so awe-inspiring that this room currently contains so *much*. Information and stories and ideas and..." I trail off, feeling a little embarrassed myself now. I got carried away.

But he looks at me with warm understanding in his gaze. "Yes. And the possibilities—don't forget those. There's already so much here, but it's also going to inspire more." He nods toward the children's section. "That's why it's so important we teach the young how to read and process what they're learning."

God and goddess, it would be so easy to fall in love with this man. I clear my throat to keep myself from asking him to marry me. "I agree," I say instead. "The café is toward the back."

Once we've found a table—it's usually busy here in the evenings, because college kids come to study while drinking their dozenth espresso drink of the day, plus the store hosts a few different book clubs—I ask him what he'd like to drink and then go to order.

When I get back with an order number and the barista's assurance that she'll bring our drinks right over, Raðulfr is reading the flyer that lists all the store's upcoming events. "This is wonderful," he says without looking up. "There's something for everyone. What a great way to build a community."

"Isn't it? I don't come to a regular book club here, but I enjoy some of their special events." I tap the line announcing a book signing with one of my favorite fiction authors. "Like this."

Before I can lift my hand away, he captures it in his and

raises it so he can examine my fingers—my paint-stained fingers. I try not to squirm.

"It *is* paint," he exclaims. "I wondered. Are you an artist?"

Oh boy. If that's what he's expecting, this is probably going to be a letdown for him. "No, I teach kindergarten. We had an incident today, where somehow one of my students got into the paint I used on the backdrop for our holiday concert. It's a little less washable than what they use for their art, so while I was cleaning up, it ended up staining me." I grimace. It's going to be a while until I can get the last of it off the table and chair Kole was using too.

"Kindergarten?" Raðulfr repeats. "That must be so rewarding—paint mishaps aside. All those curious little minds so excited about every new thing they learn."

"It *is* rewarding, though sometimes it's like herding cats who've been playing in a catnip patch." I'm glad he's not one of those people who thinks I play with the kids all day and they practically look after themselves. "I especially love this time of year, when they've mostly mastered their letters and are beginning to read bits and pieces. It's like watching them unlock a door to a new world, you know?"

He smiles at me. "Yes, I know."

Our gazes lock, and for a long second, I can't catch my breath.

"Lemongrass tea?"

Blinking, I glance up at the barista holding two mugs with teabag strings dangling over the sides.

"Oh, uh..." Shit, Raðulfr is still holding my hand. Is he *holding* it, or did he just forget he had it?

Before I can decide whether or not it would be awkward for me to pull away, he lets go. I try not to be disappointed, but I don't know what to do with my hand right now. I fiddle awkwardly with the chain that holds my amethyst pendant.

"That's mine, thank you," he says, sitting back so she can set the mug down.

"And Earl Grey for you," she announces, putting it in front of me. "Anything else I can get you?"

"No, thank you. This is perfect," I tell her, and then wait for her to leave before saying to Raðulfr, "So, uh... what is it you do? When you're not helping others learn magic, I mean."

He casts a quick glance at the tables around us, surprising me. Does it bother him that someone might have heard me say that and know he's... Well, I don't know for certain that he's Wiccan, but I'd say he's some form of pagan, given the attitudes most modern religions have toward magic use. Is he unable to practice openly? Maybe because of his job or family?

"I work in government," he says, partially answering my unasked questions. Government departments can't legally discriminate based on religious affiliation or practices, but depending on the government, they can sure as hell make things difficult. "Management. It's one of those jobs where either things are happening all at once, or nothing's happening at all."

"Not like teaching kindergarten, then," I say wryly. "Little kids can turn the most mundane thing into a parade-worthy event." My tone is light, but somehow, the easiness we had before is gone. I feel super awkward, a reaction to the combination of the hand-holding incident and him not seeming comfortable discussing magic in public. I fiddle with my pendant chain again, glancing away.

"What is that?" he asks, and I look back to see him reaching toward me.

"Uh..."

His hand stops a few inches from my collarbone. "Is it a necklace? I'm sorry—I'm being nosy."

I relax. "Nosy is my default setting, so don't worry about that. Yes, it's a necklace." I fish inside my sweater and draw out the chain and pendant for him to see. "Amethyst, for calm and peace."

He leans in to look closely. "That's stunning workmanship. Did you make it yourself?"

I laugh, because the setting around the crystal is intricate silversmithing, and the extent of my jewelry-making abilities is what the kids and I do in class. "No, I commissioned it from a silversmith—a fellow witch." I use the word deliberately, watching for his reaction, but there isn't one. Whatever caused him to worry about "magic," it doesn't apply to "witch." "They do the most stunning work."

"They do indeed," he murmurs, examining it as well as he can with it still around my neck. "I don't suppose you'd share their contact information?" He finally sits back and lifts his gaze to meet mine again.

"Of course." I slip the pendant back inside my sweater and grab my phone, feeling suddenly confident. "Here, put your number in, and I'll text you their details." I hold out my phone and add, "I promise not to misuse your number."

He takes the handset and looks me straight in the eyes as he replies, "You can use my number whenever you like."

CHAPTER SIX

Raðulfr

MY PHONE CHIMES with a message alert in the middle of a meeting with Brandt and Sam. That's not unusual—when you're the head of a government, you need to be contactable all the time. I glance down at the screen while Brandt continues to explain why it's not a bad thing that his dragons have been racing human planes. Jared's name on the screen makes me smile, and my hand twitches with the need to check the message immediately.

"...been using distortion shields every single time, and — Raðulfr, is there something you want to share?"

I jerk my head up, startled. "What?"

Curiosity is written all over Brandt's face, and there is nothing more dangerous than a curious dragon. "You're smiling."

Oh, no. "Am I not allowed to smile anymore?" I counter.

"Not when you're about to admit it's okay for dragons to race planes as long as they're not seen." He stares me down. "You're hiding something."

"I wasn't going to admit that, and yes, of course I am.

Just like you are. We don't tell each other everything, Brandt. Be reasonable." I try to sound exasperated.

"If we could get back to the matter at hand," Sam suggests, but it's too late. Brandt's been distracted.

"Who was that message from? The one that made you smile?" he demands. "Tell me or I'll tell Cecy that you ate her cake."

Sam and I exchange confused looks. "What cake?" Sam asks.

Brandt waves his hand dismissively. "Kethe saved her a piece of cake and someone ate it. She's been on a rampage ever since. Who sent the message?"

"Cecy was on a rampage? I don't think you have the right word." I shake my head. "She's more likely to use tears than destruction."

"Stop trying to change the subject." Brandt stands and leans across the table toward me, planting his palms on the surface. "I must know who sent that message!"

"You're the one who brought Cecy into this," I argue. I'm actually enjoying myself, which is a surprise. "The message was from one of my viceroys in Europe. She's expecting her first child. Is that not reason enough for me to smile?" I *did* get that message, but it was yesterday.

Brandt straightens and collapses back into his chair. "Oh. That's nice—please pass my congratulations to her. But seriously, Raðulfr, why couldn't it have been something truly interesting? Even a funny joke would have been welcome."

"This is going to be another meeting where we don't stick to the agenda, isn't it?" Sam muses. I shoot him a commiserating smile. We're both used to Brandt's idiosyncrasies, but somehow they still always manage to take us by surprise. Dragons are good at that.

"You're mostly the person who sends me funny jokes," I point out. "But if it will make you happy, I can ask my team to source some for the next meeting."

He rolls his eyes and pouts as only a thirty-thousand-year-old dragon can. "That takes all the fun out of it. How can we have been friends this long without you having learned how to be fun?"

"I feel like I should stand up for those of us who *are* fun, but just not on a dragon or hellhound level," Sam says.

"Thank you. Alistair still being Alistair?" I ask, and he shrugs.

"I'm used to it."

"Why are you both changing the subject?" Brandt demands. "We were talking about how to make Raðulfr's life more interesting!"

I blink. "We most certainly were *not*, thank you very much. My life is just fine. But now you need to finish telling us about Cecy's rampage, because I refuse to believe that precious baby actually rampaged."

"Me too," Sam agrees. "Last time I saw her, she offered me a kiss if I'd give her the ornamental letter opener from my desk. I said no, because it might not be sharp but it's still not toddler safe, and she gave me big sad eyes and a quivery lower lip."

I chuckle knowingly. "You surrendered immediately, didn't you?" It's hard to say no to Cecy's sad face.

"We compromised," Sam informs us loftily. "She could look at and touch it, but only while I was holding it."

Brandt slow claps. "Well done. Not many people can hold out against her even that much."

"So... rampage?" I prompt, and he sighs.

"You're right, it's not exactly a destructive rampage. She's just refusing to talk to anyone or play with anyone and keeps giving us the sad face. Sophie thinks she's torturing us all until her betrayer—whoever ate the cake—reveals themselves and makes it up to her."

I tip my head to one side. "Why do you sound proud?"

His smile breaks free. "Don't tell Percy, but I *am*. She's so clever. If she can keep this up, she'll get her way. Steffen's already promised to set up security cameras around the fridge so this can never happen again." He shakes his head admiringly. "She's got him wrapped around her baby claws."

Knowing Steffen, I'm not sure if that's a good thing or not. I return my attention to the question looming large in my mind. "You ate the cake, didn't you?"

Brandt gasps. "How could you accuse me of such a thing?"

Sam sighs. "He ate the cake."

"You should be ashamed," I chide. "Stealing cake from your toddler daughter—and then making everyone in the house live through your punishment."

"I don't know what you're talking about."

I grin. "Wait until I tell Steffen."

The wingleader of all dragons begins to sputter, and I sit back, satisfied that he'll never even remember the way I smiled about a text message. Not that it would really have mattered if I told Brandt and Sam that it was from Jared... and who Jared is. It's not like it's a secret that I had tea with one of the humans learning to use magic—my whole security team knows, thanks to Ari.

They don't know about the text messages, though. It's been five days since Jared and I met, and not a single one has passed without us texting each other.

First, he sent me the contact information for his silversmith, and I replied with a thank-you. The next morning, I impulsively sent a message to say I hoped his students didn't get into any more paint. It took off from there, and we've been chatting about books, plants, magic, and things that happen at work (his work stories are much better than mine, possibly because I can't tell him the really good ones). Last night he called me to say he'd over-ordered Dahlia tubers, and did I want some? I said of course, and then we talked for an hour about... stuff.

It's been a long time since I was able to talk so easily with someone I barely know.

I tune back into the conversation to find that Sam has soothed Brandt's indignation and is insisting that Brandt will definitely have to stop the plane races before an accident happens. "Even the most careful dragon can't be sure that the wind won't knock the plane sideways—or that the pilot is a good one," he's saying.

I bite back a smile at the way he avoids adding that the very, very few "careful" dragons who exist would never race a plane anyway.

ONCE I'M BACK in my office with the door closed, I finally unlock my phone and read the message.

JARED:

> I forgot to ask last night when you want to collect the tubers. Or I can bring them to you? Whatever's easiest.

Yes! I can see him again. I start typing a reply—whenever he wants—but then stop. He can't bring them to me. At home, I'd need to find a way to explain the bodyguard on duty—not to mention listen to said bodyguard's lecture about inviting strange humans into my home—and we try not to invite humans to the office without scheduling a time with security and sending out a mass email to all staff beforehand, warning them not to do anything that might give us away. I can't do that just so Jared can drop off some tubers. The questions I'd face would be horrific.

I drum my fingers on the surface of my desk. I could pick the tubers up from him, but it's unlikely that anyone on the security team is going to be happy about me going to his house, especially since I'd make them wait outside... a block away.

RAÐULFR:

> I can work around your schedule. Another visit to the bookstore?

I want to suggest lunch or dinner, but I'm trying to ease my security into the idea of Jared being in my life.

I'm trying to ease *me* into the idea of Jared being in my life. Am I really thinking about doing this? Could Jared be interested in me that way, and could something come of it? It's been so long since I was in a relationship that I'm not sure I remember how to be in one.

My phone vibrates in my hand, and I glance at the screen.

JARED:

> Perfect. Does tomorrow afternoon at four work?

I'll make it work. I send back an affirmative, hesitate, then add:

> Could I call you later? My colleague told me a story about his toddler today that I think will both horrify and amuse you.

Perhaps I should feel some sort of moral quandary about using Cecy as an excuse to get closer to a man, but I don't. It's just a story, after all.

JARED:

> Haha most toddler stories are like that! Can't wait to hear it. Talk to you later x

My breath catches as I stare at that x. I've lived on Earth for well over a decade, and I've embraced as many aspects of modern technology as I can. I know an x means a kiss.

But I also know that it's not always used to mean a *kiss*. Is this a "friendly air-kiss to end the conversation" x, or is it Jared's way of signaling that he's interested in more? I need more information.

Ten minutes on Google isn't helpful. The internet is vastly divided on this subject, and context seems to be the key factor. I need a personal consult with someone who's dated more recently than me, and more importantly, who's familiar with these Earth rituals. Brandt, maybe? Or better yet, Percy... though as I understand it, he was single for decades before he met Brandt. And neither one of them would give an opinion without asking a dozen or so questions.

Picking up my office handset, I dial a three-digit code.

"Reception, this is Dáithí." He sounds distracted, and I begin to second-guess this action.

"Dáithí, it's Raðulfr. Is this a bad time?"

"Of course not, Your Majesty. I was just typing an

email warning people not to order any more singing telegrams unless they want to feel my wrath."

He... "What?"

"Just something the dragons have been doing to amuse their very tiny minds, sir. They write the song lyrics themselves, and none of them have any talent. What can I help you with?"

I make a mental note to bring this up with Brandt. Hopefully he's not participating. "It's not important. I've received a text message from a... friend. Er... a friendly acquaintance. I mean—"

"Someone you've been flirting with. Go on."

We really don't pay him enough. "This is strictly confidential, Dáithí. I haven't decided yet if I want to pursue things. Nobody knows I'm considering it."

He pauses. "Not even Eoin?"

I knew that would get his attention. I'm not certain what's going on between the two of them—enemies, lovers, something in between—but it's been amusing the office for some time now, and Dáithí never hesitates to get one up on Eoin.

"Not even him. The security team knows about this man's existence, but that's all."

"They won't hear anything more from me." His glee makes me smile.

"Thank you. As I said, it's not important. I just want to be certain I'm interpreting something in this message correctly. He said 'talk to you later' and then ended it with an x."

"An x like a—"

"Yes. Is that... Do you think that might mean something? Or is he just signing off?"

Dáithí makes a humming sound. "Honestly, it could go

either way, but if I had to choose, I'd say he meant something. Have you been texting a lot? Flirting?"

I consider. "We met five days ago and have texted every day since. I'm not sure if we're flirting, exactly."

"Every day? Is he someone you need to be in contact with for work?"

"No."

His delighted laugh is the answer to my question. "He's into you, sir. If you've been texting every day and he's signing off with a kiss, he's trying to send you signals."

"You're sure?" Hope and insecurity war inside me.

"As sure as I can be with what I know. Let's face it, you're hot, kind, and nice to talk to. He'd be an idiot not to be interested."

Heat flushes my face. "That's... uh..."

"Don't get shy, sir. Start planning your move. I want to hear all the details when you two hook up!"

I can't believe I'm going to say this, but, "You'll be the first to know."

CHAPTER SEVEN

Jared

I STROLL into the store fifteen minutes early and glance around. It's busier than it was last week, but that's to be expected at this time of day. I don't see Raðulfr—early—so I wander toward the gardening section to see if there's anything new.

"Hi, Jared," the college student behind the counter calls as I pass, and I flip her a wave.

"Hey, Beth. Great shirt." It says, "I like my whiskey straight, but my friends can go either way." She grins at me and turns her attention to an approaching customer.

I'm pretending to look at a book about container planting but really wondering if Raðulfr is just coming to collect the tubers or might also want to hang out with me, when the skin along my neck starts to crawl. I glance around, but nothing seems out of place—just a bunch of people browsing, and some happy chatter coming from the café. My instinct doesn't usually—

Is that woman staring at me?

I glance over my shoulder to see if she's looking at something behind me—maybe she's reading a poster.

There's nothing there but a wall of books, so unless she has fantastic eyesight and can read the spines from a dozen feet away, she's staring at me… and her expression isn't the friendliest. She's standing beside the self-help section, not even pretending to be interested in books, and looks like she's sizing me up.

Should I be worried? My instincts say no—in fact, now that I've noticed her watching me, they don't seem concerned about her in the slightest. Sometimes I wonder if there's any point to having good instincts if they can't give me any real information.

"Jared?"

I look away from the woman and see Raðulfr walking down the aisle toward me, a smile on his face, and I can't stop myself from smiling back. "Hi. I was just browsing." I put the container gardening book back on the shelf.

"Really?" he asks with a teasing note. "Because it seemed like you were staring into space."

Chuckling, I pull a rueful face. "Yeah… well, no. Not to sound conceited or anything, but I thought that woman might be staring at me, and I was trying to work out why." I gesture vaguely in the direction of the woman, who's still watching.

Raðulfr glances that way, and his lips tighten just the tiniest bit. "I bet she's jealous of your hair," he declares. "It's so curly and healthy."

I blink. She's… what? "Uh…"

"Ignore her. Do you know where the section on parenting is? I want to get my friend a book—kind of a joke, since he thinks it's funny that his daughter rules the house."

Letting myself be distracted, I lead him toward the right area—it's one I'm familiar with, since it includes all the books about early childhood development. "Is this the friend who told you the horrifyingly amusing story?"

"Yes! It all started when Brandt—my friend—ate some cake that was being saved for her..." He launches into the story, and he's right about it being funny and also terrifying.

"That kid is going to rule the world one day," I predict, and for some reason, he winces.

"She's certainly going to have her family under her thumb," he agrees.

We wander through the shelves for almost an hour, talking about books and friends and work, and then end up in the café once the after-school crowd starts to thin out.

"Tell me about Wicca," he says, tapping the cover of the book on top of the stack I've gathered, and I sputter, taken aback.

"You don't... I'm sorry. I guess I just assumed you already knew about... I mean, with the magic and all." He flinches just like last time when I say "magic," and I wish I knew what that was about. Why does that one word worry him?

He takes a sip from his drink, then explains, "My family is a different branch of pagan. You might have guessed from my accent that I'm not from around here. Where I used to live, we didn't learn a lot about religions and other practices... not recently, anyway. I've been meaning to do some reading on the subject since I came here, but time is a commodity that always seems to escape me." He shrugs. "Some colleagues of mine have talked a lot about Wicca and other hu— religious practices, and it all sounds beautiful. You have gods, don't you?"

"The god and goddess," I correct. "Although our relationship with them is different from many other religions, and our worship tends to be a lot more personal and less... communal."

Raðulfr props his elbows on the tabletop and leans forward. "What does that mean? Less communal?"

He seems genuinely interested and not at all judgy, so I relax a little. "No churches, for one. Some do choose to gather for special ceremonies—solstice or equinox, to name the biggest—and some witches are most comfortable as part of a coven, but not all."

"Are you?" He shakes his head. "I'm sorry—is it okay for me to ask that?"

"I don't mind," I assure him. "I think we're good enough friends to ask the occasional personal question—don't you?" My heartbeat picks up as I realize that I could have phrased that better. What if he thinks it means I only want to be friends?

His lovely gray eyes meet mine, and he says hesitantly, "I think we could venture beyond friendship, if we both wanted to."

Giddy excitement bursts inside me, and I smile so wide my cheeks feel like they might crack. "Me too."

We sit there grinning foolishly at each other for a moment, and then I pull myself together. "Uh, so... no, I don't have a coven. I considered it when I first started practicing—most witches come to Wicca through mentorship by another witch, and mine was part of a great coven. They were very welcoming and offered me a place with them, but it never quite fit. I think I'm more of a solitary witch. They still invite me to join them sometimes, and I'll go, or I meet up with some other solitary witches." I pick up my mug and sip my coffee—I have some lesson planning to do tonight, so the caffeine is needed.

"I like that," he muses. "That your religion is something so deeply personal, to be shared only if and when you want, and that there's no judgment or expectation from other practitioners for your choice."

I snort. "Oh, we have plenty of expectations and the occasional judgment," I correct. "But not how you mean. Some people might judge me for not being in a coven, might think I'm missing part of the experience, but it's their personal opinion and not anything else. We all have our preferred ways of doing things, and of course everyone thinks their way is the right way, but mostly, the only expectation Wicca has—the only real rule—is that we do no harm. We do not use our gifts from nature to cause hurt to others."

He nods. "That's a rule I also live by. We have so very much in common. Were you raised Wiccan?"

Shaking my head, I glance away. "No. I came to it when I was already an adult. My family was—is—Christian, and their church isn't... well, it's not accepting of anything that doesn't fit a very rigid perspective." I stop, because he doesn't need my whole life story—not yet.

But his gaze is far too perceptive. "They hurt you deeply," he murmurs, and I nod helplessly.

"Yeah. For a lot of reasons. I don't have contact with them anymore, and although that makes me sad sometimes, it's more because I miss having a family than because I regret cutting ties. My phone number and email address are the same, so if they'd changed, they could have reached out. The silence means they haven't, and I don't need to be part of something that was so harmful for me."

Reaching across the table, Raðulfr covers my hand with his, just for a moment. "I'm glad you have the strength to know that, though I'm sorry that you have to."

It's the best thing he could have said. "Thank you. What about your family—I know you learned magic from a young age, but have they been supportive of... everything?"

The solemn moment dispelled, Raðulfr sits back. "Oh, yes. I had two sisters, one older and one younger, and my grandfather came to live with us when I was small. My parents were both musicians, and any time one of us complained about lessons or chores, they'd find a way to set it to music. I can't even remember how many times I tidied my bedchamber to a three/four count."

A laugh escapes me. "How would that even work? I mean... I'm not completely sure what that *is*."

"Maybe one day I can demonstrate," he suggests. "Though I haven't done it for a very long time. It did help to make things fun, though, if only because we were so busy laughing or rolling our eyes at our parents that we forgot to be petulant."

"I can't imagine you ever being petulant. Peevish, maybe," I tease, still excited by the idea that he might help me clean a room in my house someday. That's intimate—well, it is for me, anyway. I don't invite a lot of people to even visit my house, much less make themselves at home.

"I can be petulant," he assures me. "Peevish, too. Though I'm not very often, these days. My life is happy, so I don't have much call to be."

"I like to look on the positive side of things too." Our gazes meet again, another drawn-out moment that makes me feel all the excited tingles inside. I can't remember the last time I had this kind of reaction to someone, and I didn't realize how much I missed it. When did my relationships become so low-key and transactional? "Did your family move to America too, or do they still—I'm sorry, I don't think I caught where you lived before?"

Sadness crosses his handsome face. "They died. My younger sister first, then my mother. My father chose not to continue without her. They loved each other so deeply, you see. My older sister was the last to be lost." He shakes his head and adds, almost absently, "I tried so hard, but nothing I did stopped it."

Clearly he blames himself for their deaths, though I can't imagine why. It sounds like they might have lived in a conflict zone? I'm not going to push for more information when it upsets him.

Repeating his gesture of not long ago, I reach across the table and cover his hand with mine. "I'm so sorry. They sound like they were amazing people."

His smile returns, sadder and simpler, but still there. "They were. The best. I hope to meet them again in future lives."

"I'm sure you will. We're drawn to the souls we loved in the past."

"We are," he says, turning his hand under mine so they're palm-to-palm. "It's a true joy."

We're basically just holding hands and staring at each other, but I wouldn't give this moment up. Such a simple connection and yet—

Something bounces off the side of Raðulfr's head. Blinking, I let go of his hand as we both lean to look down at the floor. It's a wadded-up piece of napkin.

"What...?" I turn to scan the side of the room it must have come from, looking for kids or even teenagers who might be responsible, but the only occupied tables have adults. Who would—

"Is that the same woman who was staring before?"

Surely she didn't throw a napkin at us. She's not even looking at us anymore.

"Maybe," Raðulfr says, his eyes narrowed in her direction. "Never mind. I suppose it's not a terrible thing that we were interrupted. I've been here longer than I planned."

I glance at my watch and wince. "Me too. I was having too good a time. We could do it again soon?"

That easily, he forgets about the woman, turning instead to smile warmly at me. "We will."

WHEN THE KNOCK comes at my office door the next morning, I'm ready for it. Eoin may think he's in charge of this meeting he called to lecture me on security and humans, but he's wrong.

"Enter." I rest my hands on the top of my desk and don my stern expression. It's gotten me through many situations that were much more difficult than this.

The head of my security team lets himself in and closes the door before he turns to see my face. "Not having a good morning, Your Majesty?" he asks.

"It hasn't been too bad, but we have some serious issues to discuss."

He hovers for a moment, waiting for me to stand and invite him over to the armchairs where we normally have our meetings. I see the actual moment when he realizes what my failure to do so means. His eyelid twitches, and he slides into one of the visitor chairs facing my desk. "We do, Your Majesty. The team has raised some serious safety concerns."

"I'm sure they have. Please, do share them." Aside

from a moment where I nearly slipped up and called Wicca a *human* religious practice—which it is, but the implication would have raised questions—I haven't done anything to truly raise concern.

Eoin sighs, the way he always does when he thinks I'm being difficult. The fact that he's only had to do it a handful of times in the past thousand years gives a good picture of how easy I am to look after. I should get a free pass to be "difficult" every once in a while.

"I was surprised when Niamh reported that your meeting yesterday afternoon was with the same human you went out with after the magic class last week," he begins.

"Were you? I'm surprised that it's important enough to surprise you."

He sighs again, and I resist the inappropriate urge to smile. I've never made him sigh at me twice in one meeting—and for it to happen within just a few minutes! Maybe Brandt's recklessness has finally rubbed off on me. "Everything you do is important to your security team," he declares. I'd feel guilty—as he clearly intends—except I've done nothing to put my safety at risk. "Which is why we're concerned that you've been keeping secrets from us."

Taken aback, I say, "Excuse me?"

"Your first meeting with the human was impulsive and perhaps misguided. This second meeting, however, was obviously arranged ahead of time, which means you've been corresponding with the human."

"His name is Jared." This conversation is far worse than I had expected, but one thing I want to be clear on from the outset is that nobody will disrespect Jared. "And yes, he and I have been in communication this past week. I've also communicated with all my viceroys, Brandt,

Percy, and several others—do you require a comprehensive list? I don't have one ready, because it has never been of interest to you before."

"Surely you can understand why this is different," Eoin begins, but I don't see this conversational gambit going anywhere that would be acceptable to me.

"No, actually. Thanks to Steffen, Jared has undergone a deeper background and security assessment than some of the people who have access to walk into this office. It's been determined by a combined security panel—to which you appointed a member—that he is not a person who would do harm to the community even if he should accidentally discover the truth. He has been deemed safe to teach magic to. I fail to understand why you believe, given all this, that me exchanging text messages with him poses a security risk."

Eoin's lips tighten. "Niamh's report—"

"Ah, yes. Let's go on a little tangent, shall we? Perhaps you can explain to me why you're lecturing me about security when Niamh posed a far greater risk to it last night than I did?"

He straightens. "What do you mean?"

"The first thing we agreed to do when we migrated here was fly under the radar and avoid arousing human suspicions," I remind him, and he nods. "Standing in the middle of a store and blatantly staring at a human for uninterrupted minutes is *not* inconspicuous. Jared was uncomfortable. We're fortunate that he wasn't so uncomfortable as to report it to the staff, who might have called the police. I'm sure having my bodyguard escorted from the store by the police wouldn't have been conspicuous *at all*."

"I wasn't aware—"

"Then," I continue, "shortly before I departed the

store, Niamh thought the best way to get my attention would be to throw a napkin at my head. Jared saw her and recognized her as the person who'd made him uncomfortable earlier. It's fortunate that I distracted him before he put the details together and realized that she not only was the one who threw the napkin"—I inject those three words with disgust—"but also that she's connected to *me*." I told Niamh last night that I wasn't happy with her professionalism, so she won't be surprised when Eoin raises this with her.

"Niamh told me about the napkin," Eoin admits. He doesn't sound any happier about it than me. "I agree it wasn't advisable—especially since the h— Jared had seen her earlier and recognized her. She says it was the least objectionable and noticeable way for her to prevent you from potentially taking an unsafe physical action."

I've been around for a long time and am widely considered to be wise, intelligent, and knowledgeable, yet it still takes me a moment to process and understand that sentence. "I thought I knew Niamh fairly well," I say slowly, "but is it possible I missed the fact that she's homophobic?"

"Raðulfr," Eoin chides. He only calls me by name when he's particularly exasperated. "You know that's not true."

"I didn't think it was, but I can't imagine why else she'd think me holding a man's hand might lead to—what did you call it? 'Unsafe physical action.'" Disappointment is a lead weight in my stomach. Does my security team not want me to find happiness again?

"It's not that Jared is a man."

"Then what? We've already established that he's met security standards."

"He's *human*," Eoin grinds out. "And before you accuse

me of being speciesist, I'd like you to seriously think about this. Our—*your*—entire existence is a secret from him. He thinks you're human like him. You could never truly be honest, be yourself with him. He doesn't even know what you really look like."

Involuntarily, I lift a hand to the side of my face. The difference in bone structure between elves and humans is enough that we use spellcraft to hide it—along with our pointy ears. It's true; Jared has only seen my glamor.

Eoin presses on. "We were mildly concerned yesterday when it seemed like you'd befriended him, but when Niamh reported the hand-holding and calf-eyed looks, that concern became a very real thing. Are you romantically interested in this man, Your Majesty? And if you are, why did you keep it from us?"

"It's only been a week, and we've only been texting," I defend. "If I'd decided to pursue this, I would have advised you."

"If you'd decided to pursue this?" he echoes. "Respectfully, sir, have I been talking to myself for the past ten minutes? You *can't* pursue this. He's human, and he knows nothing about us."

I narrow my eyes. This conversation is truly beginning to irritate me now. "The community has welcomed trustworthy humans for thousands of years, Eoin. Humans marry into all species—it's how we were able to begin the program to reintroduce magic to them."

"Yes, but none of them has married a species leader before."

The words fall between us like stones, shocking me.

"You are not just any member of the community, Your Majesty. Nearly two hundred thousand elves rely on you to guide us and be our connection to the life force. If you pursued things with this man, not only would you be forced to be dishonest with him in the early part of your relationship, but when—if—you eventually revealed the truth, you'd also have to tell him that he'd be sharing your time and attention with your people. That his life would come under scrutiny for being with you. That's a lot of pressure, and I'd hate to see you hurting again, sir."

I say nothing. Eoin doesn't pull his punches when he has a point to make.

After a moment, he stirs. "I wish we hadn't had to have this conversation," he says softly. "Your safety and well-being are my priority, sir, and have been for a long time. That's not just physical. All of us on the team care about you, and we want what's best for you. If you choose to pursue things with the human—Jared—that's your choice to make, and we'll all wish you every happiness. We just want to ensure you've considered every aspect of it."

He said a moment ago that he would hate to see me hurting again, but it might be too late for that. All the excitement and joy that's been fizzing inside me for the last week, and especially since last night, is gone, flattened by the gloom of reality. Even if things between Jared and me do continue to grow, it's a rare man who would stand fast under the revelations that his partner was lying to him, was of a different, previously unknown to him species, and was in a high-pressure leadership role with no retirement in sight. Is Jared one of those rare men? Do I want to potentially put myself through the pain of discovering he isn't?

My phone chimes, as if on cue, and because I desperately need the distraction, I pick it up and swipe to read the message.

JARED:

Good morning! I was thinking… Do you want to come over this weekend? There's a new moon Sunday night, and I wanted to add some magic to some of my usual rituals. You can learn more about Wicca and we can work on some spells together. I'll even feed you LOL.

I stare at the message for a long moment, my heart aching, then text back:

Yes, please.

Raising my eyes to Eoin, I say, "I don't know yet what I'm going to do, but I'm taking a few days to think about it, and I'm having dinner with Jared at his home on Sunday."

My head of security tightens his lips. "That sounds like you've made a decision."

"No." I shake my head. "It's not that easy. But by Sunday, I'll know whether I'm going to use this dinner to say goodbye or not." My tone is grim, because I know what I need to do. Maybe I'm delaying, but it would be foolish of me to do anything except end this infatuation.

Eoin nods. "It would be helpful if you could find out his address ahead of time so—"

"You're not going into his home while he's not there," I order. "We've established that he's trustworthy. It's bad enough that I'll have a bodyguard sitting outside the whole time." I'm not letting them violate his private space, not when I know from things he's said how fiercely he guards it.

From the expression on his face, Eoin's not happy. That makes two of us.

I RING the doorbell of the charming cottage that's Jared's home. His front garden is tiny, just a patch, really, but even in winter it's tidy, and I can tell from the dormant plants that it will be lovely in just a few short weeks.

Too bad I won't be around to see it then. I've been psyching myself up to do the right thing for days, and it's made me miserable. The only times I've let myself be happy are when Jared and I are talking on the phone—and that makes things even worse, because how can I say goodbye to something with so much promise?

The door opens, warm light and the lovely lemony scent I already associate with Jared flooding out to envelop me, and Jared smiles at me with such pleasure that my resolve wavers.

Something brushes against my ankle, and I look down at the cat winding its way between my feet.

"Oh—sorry," Jared says. "That's Marge. I forgot to ask if you were allergic or anything."

I bend and scoop the cat up, cradling her in my arms. "No, I'm not allergic."

Jared beams. "Good. Because Margie's queen around here, and we would have had to spend the whole night outside if you were."

The life force rushes around me, a whirling, dizzying burst of etheric energy, the way it always is when it wants to communicate something to me. Realization settles in my bones. Eoin's probably going to sigh, but I'm not giving up Jared... not unless he wants me to.

CHAPTER NINE

Jared

SEEING Raðulfr and Marge instantly take to each other makes my inner self do a little happy dance. I'm not much of a dancer, so it's more of an arms-flailing-wriggle-and-hip-bump than anything else, but it counts. My instincts were spot-on about asking Raðulfr over, even though I've only met him twice in person. I'm getting seriously good vibes about him and our future relationship.

The vibes increase when he stops in the entryway and toes off his shoes without me needing to ask him. I don't always ask my few guests to take their shoes off—I know it makes some of them uncomfortable—but I always notice the ones who do it anyway because they care about *my* comfort.

"This is charming," Raðulfr says as he follows me into the living room. "There's so much character and love here. It must give you so much pleasure to come home to this every day."

I smile over my shoulder at him. "It does, and thank you. I've worked hard to make it a haven for myself. Please sit down and be comfortable. We have a few minutes before we need to begin."

He sits on the right side of the couch—not that there are a lot of places for him to choose from—and settles Marge in his lap for more pets and scratches. She blinks slowly at me, blissed out.

I take the opposite end of the couch, which, considering its size, leaves only a few inches between us, and tuck my feet up as I turn toward him. I've already bathed ahead of the ritual and am dressed in the white cotton pants I always wear, plus a long-sleeved blue tee, the color chosen to hopefully help in boosting my psychic aware-ness. I'm planning to use at least one of the minor magics I've learned during the ritual—likely more. Just for the candles, mostly, and perhaps setting up the altar.

"Tell me what tonight entails. You said it was the new moon?" he asks, eyes attentive on my face, and I nod.

"Yes. Astronomically, it's in about twenty minutes, so I'd like to time the ritual to begin then or shortly after. The new moon is a time of new beginnings and energy. It's an excellent time to set intentions and begin projects and... other things." Like relationships. I figure it can't hurt to use the power of the new moon to attract the goddess's energy to what I hope is happening between me and Raðulfr.

"How does the ritual work?" He's still petting Margie, and the half-asleep happy sounds she's making indicate she won't give him up anytime soon.

"I'd like to do this one outside—that's usually my pref-erence, when the weather permits. I know it's cold tonight, but it's not freezing and there's no snow or rain, so..."

Raðulfr shakes his head, a faint smile on his face.

"Please don't feel you need to justify yourself to me. It's so much easier for me to feel the universe's energy when I'm outdoors. And I have a coat." He stops. "Unless you'd rather I stay inside and watch from here? I'm not sure how involved you'd like me to be."

"You can come outside with me," I hurry to assure him, wondering if I've made a mistake after all, "if you want to. I thought maybe this first time, you could watch? There's nothing stopping non-Wiccans from participating, so you could do that if you wanted, but—"

"I'd prefer to observe tonight, if that's okay," he interrupts calmly. "You said last week that this was personal for you. I'm very honored to be here at all, and until I understand better, I'd rather not overstep. Is there anything I need to do to prepare?"

Calm seeps back through me, my instincts stirring smugly to remind me that they were right about him. "As a watcher, no." There's no negative energy clinging to him that I can sense. Some residual emotional turmoil—perhaps the thing that's been distracting him for the past few days? But whatever the problem was, it's been solved. "Once we're outside, I'll create the circle and set up the altar for the ritual." I hesitate. "You won't be able to cross inside the circle."

"An energy barrier?" He tilts his head. "That's fascinating. We use those when experimenting with bigger spells. They act as containment and protection."

My smile is instant. "Yes, exactly. Ours is to protect the sacred space during the ritual. I suppose some things are universal among practitioners of magic. Once the circle is closed, I'll call the four elements, ask nature and the goddess for their blessing, and make my offering. Then I'll open the circle, and we can come inside for dinner." I sound a little uncertain on the last few words. Could I have made it sound any more prosaic? I mean, it *is*, but it's also an important spiritual ritual that means a lot to me.

"I can't wait to see it," Raðulfr says. "Shall we go outside? Or is there something you need to do first?"

I stand, energy already racing through me. "Let's go—that is, if the queen will let you."

"She's not allowed out?" He carefully gets to his feet without disturbing her in his arms, and he's a lot more graceful about it than I usually am.

"She's allowed in the back garden, because the fence is too high for her, but she doesn't like being left out of the circle, so she's begun shunning ritual time entirely. Maybe with you for company, she might want to join us." We go back to the front door to collect coats and shoes, and then into the kitchen, where the door into the back garden is.

"Is there a reason she can't be in the circle?" Raðulfr asks as he shifts Marge from one arm to the other so I can help him get his coat on.

I shrug and snort. "No, except that she sometimes gets bored. I've had to rescue the ritual candles from her a few times, and once she tried to eat the flowers I'd laid on the altar. It was just easier to start leaving her outside it."

His chuckle as I open the door is a warm contrast to the cold air that meets us. "She and I will just keep cuddling, then." He follows me outside and looks around. It's dark, but I installed dozens of small solar lights that give the courtyard a warm glow and provide enough light to see by. There's a floodlight, too, but I don't like to use it that much. "This is lovely, Jared. So tranquil."

My cheeks get hot, but it doesn't stop my grin. I've worked hard to make this garden what I need it to be—my own oasis. "Thank you. Over this way." I gesture past the herb planters I use for the more invasive plants—things like mint, which are lovely to have around, but tend to take over and choke out their neighbors. I've utilized almost every inch of space in this garden, but there's a narrow path of paving stones that a neighbor gave me when she landscaped her front yard. They were cracked and broken, so she was replacing them, but using the cracks to reshape them and laying them as stepping stones rather than as a solid path has given them a new lease on life. They're the most gorgeous dark gray streaky granite—I couldn't let them go to landfill.

The path takes us past the herb garden to the space under my one full-sized tree, a stately old oak. Its branches are bare right now, but in summer it provides lovely shade for the bench I've positioned under it. This part of the garden is dedicated to my "pleasure plants," the ones purely for joy, though most of them are dormant at this time of year.

There is a clear space, however, and this is where I have my circle. I've planted out a five-foot diameter of space with clover, giving me a tiny lawn of sorts, and bordered it with sage, giving the circle a permanent physical presence in my garden.

"Oh," Raðulfr says, his surprise clear. "It's an actual circle."

I set down the plastic tub with my things in it and turn to face him. "Yes. It doesn't have to be, of course. This"—I wave to my clover-and-sage patch—"is just planting. I like this spot, and it seemed sensible to set it up the way that suits me best."

"I agree. I especially like that you've used clover and not grass. Much better for the bees and other pollinators, especially in such a busy garden." He looks around again in the cozy glow of the lights. "It really is special. I hope one day you'll invite me to see it by daylight."

Maybe tomorrow morning. I blush. That wasn't... I didn't invite him here intending for him to stay over. He needs to stop being so amazing.

"I will," I manage. "Um, you can sit over there, if you like. Or you can stand wherever. Obviously you can tell where the circle is, so..." I trail off and decide to move on. It's nearly time, and Raðulfr doesn't need to guess how nervous I am to have him watch me.

It's good nervous, though.

I move the container into the circle and crouch to take everything out, laying the items in the clover until the tub is empty and I can turn it upside down to use as my altar. Straightening, I consider whether I want to use my athame to cast the circle tonight. I don't need it, but if I'm putting on a show...

That thought makes up my mind. Tonight isn't about showiness—I genuinely want Raðulfr to see how the magic I'm learning works with my religion. I don't usually use the athame to cast the circle anymore, not unless I need help with focus. He'll be able to see me use it for other things in the future.

Standing, I take two steps to the northernmost point of the circle, exhale deeply, and let myself feel nature's energy flowing through me. It's so much easier now than it was when I first started. When the ebb and flow of power is a thrum in every part of my being, I lift my hand and point to the sage border. Energy spills from me, fixing to the earth, and I slowly walk the circle clockwise, trailing the energy with me until I reach the starting point and the circle has been drawn. Next, I close my eyes and visualize the energy stretching into the air above me and the earth below, until a perfect sphere has formed.

The circle is complete.

With the solid hum of it surrounding me, empowering me, I turn to the north again and call upon fire. To the east for air. South for earth, and finally west for water, sealing the circle.

I risk a quick glance at Raðulfr as I return to my altar. Fascination is all over his face as he sits on the bench mere feet away, Marge still in his arms, studying my circle. I can tell he sees it by the way his gaze tracks up over the dome above me. I guess this is another benefit of being with a magic user—he won't think I'm making up this part of my practice. I've had past partners who were supportive of my paganism, but lost patience when I talked about the magic elements of it.

Kneeling, I lay the white cloth over the container, then set out candles for the god and goddess—gold and silver, respectively, tonight, to amplify my ambition and intuition. My goals are to bring an energy boost to my new relationship and my new magic skills. Every little detail matters.

CHAPTER TEN

Raðulfr

I WATCH EAGERLY as Jared lays out the tools for his ritual. His circle is beautiful, strong and thrumming with the essence of the life force, perfectly formed. This is clearly something he's done many times, but it's not just that. The life force has a fondness for him. It's not rare for that to happen, but not common either. My experience is that those people are usually good ones.

As if to confirm my thoughts, the life force wraps itself around me in a happy little dance. It's been a part of my life like this for so long that I honestly don't know what I'll do when the time comes for it to move on to the next king or queen... although there are a lot of possibilities, things that my position has held me back from.

My eyes linger on Jared. Things like relationships. Ásta and I had been together for more than two thousand years, and married half that, when I was invested as king. It was a surprise to us both, but she rallied and was my helpmeet in every way for thousands of years of leading the elves. Until she wasn't.

Since then, things haven't aligned to give me that kind of love again. Perhaps I'm being presumptuous to think—

The life force surrounds me again with a distinct sensation of disagreement, and I tamp down the excitement that results. The future will work itself out—for now, I'll focus on the present and the delightful man before me, who's asked me to observe a very personal ritual.

Jared draws on the life force and gracefully lights both candles and then a short stick of incense, his control of the flame perfect. He places a pear, three dates, and two dried figs in a shallow bowl, then bows his head and breathes steadily, purposefully, as one would in meditation. He's centering himself, and I follow his lead and do the same. One can never have too much of a connection with nature and the world that surrounds us. I let my breathing fall into an even rhythm, tuning in to the sounds of the winter night around me, the soft sensation of Marge's fur beneath my fingers. Even the cold air that nips at my cheeks and seeps inside my coat is another link to the energy that makes up existence. Power, both my own innate source and that of the life force, sings around me, through me, but I let it flow without disturbance, merely enjoying its presence and the life it represents.

A few minutes later, Jared begins to speak softly. He's quiet enough that he likely believes I can't hear him, but in the still of the evening and with my better-than-human hearing, every word is as clear as if he were right beside me.

"In the dark of the time between,
I beseech thee, blessed goddess,
bring forth new light and new beginnings.
May the waxing strength of your moon

inform the growth of new skills and new love."

A breath catches in my throat, though thankfully he doesn't seem to hear it. I was right to come tonight. I was right to decide that I'd give things a chance between us. I was right. Surely this, plus the life force's fondness for Jared, are signs that he would accept who I am and the secrets I'm currently keeping from him?

I'll have to wait to find out. Even I know it would be foolhardy to disclose everything now. This first rush of attraction and lust may fade.

Jared sits meditatively for a few more minutes, then murmurs thanks to his goddess and god. His eyes narrow in concentration, drawing on the life force. A moment later, both candles go out.

A delighted grin spreads across my face. I helped him learn that! And he's been practicing, to be able to coordinate in two directions without a spell or anything.

He lifts his hand and gestures in a counterclockwise direction, and the circle dissipates, the energy absorbed back into nature. I stand, and Marge must decide she's had enough of me, because she stretches and jumps down from my arms, heading to the house.

Jared turns his head toward me. "I hope you weren't too bored," he says tentatively, and I shake my head.

"I wasn't bored at all. Aside from the pleasure of watching you use magic so competently and elegantly, I found the ritual itself fascinating. Is it okay for me to come there? I have some questions."

His face lights up, though he keeps his smile small. "Of course. Or we can go inside—it's always warmer in the circle, but you've been sitting in the cold."

I step inside the sage border and kneel on the clover beside him. "Let's do both. I'd like to know what all these things are for, please, and I can help you put them away while you explain. If that's okay," I add, belatedly realizing there might be a rule about other people touching some of the items.

"It's fine," he assures me, "though it's not really something that needs two people. I tend to prefer a simple altar, though there are times I feel the need for more ceremony. This," he touches a finger to the shallow bowl with the fruit in it, "is my offering to the god and goddess. It's customary to return it to the earth once the ritual is done. Some people prefer to bury it, but I think scattering it in the garden meets the same purpose." He stands gracefully, lifting the bowl, and disperses the contents under the tree. When he returns, the bowl is set aside.

"The incense is supposed to burn until it's finished," he explains, gesturing to the simple metal holder the stick is standing in. "Which is why for outdoor rituals, I cut the sticks if I think it's not going to be a long one. I don't want to be responsible for an accidental fire or for some curious animal getting burned."

"I did wonder why the stick was so short," I admit, impressed by his forethought. "That's clever. How much longer do you th—" I stop when the last remnant of the incense goes out, the rising smoke thinning to wisps and then nothing. "Nicely played."

He chuckles. "Do this enough times, and you get to be an expert. I figured I'd need about thirty minutes, and I was right."

I reach out and let my hand hover over the small piece of bamboo remaining in the holder. "May I?"

"Yeah, sure. The stick will be hot, though, so don't touch it. I'll run it in water before I recycle it."

He's so thoughtful. Carefully, I lift the holder off his

altar and place it beside the bowl. "What are the crystals for?"

Jared names each one as he picks it up. "Quartz, moonstone, aventurine, amethyst. All stones that would boost my purpose tonight. I don't always use crystals in my rituals, but sometimes they help to give me focus."

That makes sense on several levels—crystals come from the earth, and since, unlike plants, they don't die when cut from their source, they retain a connection. I don't say that, though. It would be too easy to accidentally give too much away.

"That just leaves the candles and the cloth."

"Heh, the cloth isn't important. I use it because I like it. But the candles represent the god," he points to the one on the right, then to the left and adds, "and the goddess. Or not represents them, exactly, but pays tribute to them." He adds them to the other items on the grass, then whisks away the cloth. "And as you can see, my altar when I'm out here is this very handy container that doubles as storage."

"Practical," I agree, helping as he begins packing things inside the tub. "I like that you can set your altar up anywhere. That seems far more sensible than those religions that require worship to take place in limited spaces."

"I've always liked it," he admits. "The god and goddess—the world, nature, everything—are all around us. Why should our reverence for them be restricted?"

I clamber to my feet and bend to pick up the container. "May I carry this for you?"

He smiles shyly as he rises also. "Thank you. That's kind."

We turn toward the house, and I ask, "You said earlier that the container is your altar when you're out here. Do you have a different one inside?"

He nods, leading the way past the healthy herb beds. He has an excellent late-winter crop, and I hope he'll invite me over to garden with him one day.

And that I can return the invitation. My rooftop garden might not be the one I had to leave behind on my homeworld, but it's still important to me.

"Yes, I have a permanent altar in the second bedroom. Well, semi-permanent. It's a beautiful hand-crafted wood and resin tray. It lives on top of my bookcase, and I move it around when I want to use it. I thought about buying a table and doing something actually permanent, but that would be harder to move around the house, and sometimes I want to use different rooms." He holds the door open for me, and I enter the warm kitchen. Marge is curled up on the table, watching us with unblinking eyes.

"She likes you," Jared says, following the direction of my gaze. "That's a big compliment, because she's picky." He takes the container from me and sets it on a sideboard, then goes to wash his hands at the sink.

"How long have you lived together?" I ask, following him to take a turn at the sink. I'm hoping he'll let me help with dinner.

He laughs. "I love that you phrased it that way, instead of asking when I got her. Margie chose me six years ago. I was working in the front garden, and this tiny kitten comes marching up the front path, straight to the door, and stands there mewing at it like she's demanding for it to open. I knew my neighbor's cat, across the street, had been pregnant, so I figured that's where she came from and took her back."

"And then changed your mind and decided to keep her?" I guess, leaning against the counter as he pulls a covered pot out of the fridge and sets it on the stove.

"Not likely." He snorts. "It wasn't that I was against having a pet, but I didn't have a lot of time back then to devote to one—still don't, really—and if I did, I would have adopted an older animal from a shelter. One who was less likely to find a home and already house-trained. A kitten wasn't on my radar."

I grin. That's exactly how many elves feel about their dragon friends. We love them dearly, but we're all a bit bewildered about how we happened to end up with someone so high-maintenance and... catastrophic in our friendship circle. "Yet here she is. Clearly you're not the one in charge in this house."

Shaking his head, he gets a wooden spoon from a drawer and gives whatever is warming up in that pot a stir. "I definitely am not. The next day, I found her waiting for me on the doorstep when I got home from work. I took her back again, but two days later, she was waiting when I opened the door—and that time she managed to get past me. I found her curled up on the couch, staking her claim on my house."

"Is that when you gave in?"

"Nope. By the way, I hope vegetable soup is okay for dinner? I have garlic rolls to go with it."

On cue, my stomach rumbles. "Sounds great to me. Can I help set the table?"

"Sure—I'll get things out for you. Anyway," he continues, turning to a cabinet and taking out two glasses, "after the fifth—or maybe sixth—time I took her home, my neighbor suggested it might be time I clued in that I'd been adopted. I was arguing about it when two of the other kittens from the litter ganged up on Margie. In retrospect, they were only playing, but I reacted like an overprotective parent watching their kid get beat up, and that was when I realized she and I were meant to be."

I finish laying the spoons on the table with the napkins and glasses and take the jug of water he hands me. "That's the sweetest story I've heard in a long while. How did you choose her name? That's such an important part of the pet process."

A shadow crosses his face, and I immediately wish I could snatch the question back. "She's named after my grandmother, who died when I was a kid," he says quietly. "She... well, to be honest, I don't know for sure how she would have reacted when I came out, but from what I remember of her, she had the best shot of still wanting me around. Maybe she wouldn't, but I'll never know, and I like to pretend she would have accepted me... and everything."

If it wouldn't be a horrific misuse of power, I'd ask Caolan to track down Jared's family and make sure they were suffering in some way for the harm they've done to him. But that won't take his pain away, and, knowing that he lives by the edict "do no harm," it's unlikely that he'd appreciate it.

Instead, I cross to stand directly in front of him and lift my hands to cup his cheeks. There's just a hint of beard grain under my palms, reminding me how very, very long it's been since I was last with a man. Jared's eyes search my face, his breath picking up speed just a fraction.

"I bet she would have accepted you," I promise. Whether she would have or not, if the dream he created makes him happy, I'll feed it with every ounce of my own belief. "She loved you so much, and she would have supported all your choices. Because you're incredible, and I know she recognized that the way I do."

The last word barely has time to leave my lips before his are crashing against them. He clings to my shoulders, then wraps his arms around me and hauls us against each other, pressed together from mouth to thigh, as close as we can be with our clothes between us. My lips part under the pressure of his, and the taste of him explodes through me, making me feel, for the first time in so very long, that I'm home.

CHAPTER ELEVEN

Jared

KISSING Raðulfr is like eating gourmet ice cream at the beach with your friends on a scorching hot day. It's like being wrapped in a blanket in front of the fire with your cat and a great book. It's like being on a roller coaster, screaming and laughing and never wanting the ride to end; like the first time I used magic and understood the real beauty of the world.

It feels like the best decision I've ever made.

We stand there beside the counter in my kitchen and kiss until I'm dizzy, until my lips start to feel tender and it seems like I'll never get enough of how he feels against me. Until Margie yowls and a sizzling sound tells me the soup's boiled over.

Shit.

We break apart, and I hurry to turn off the burner before it makes too much mess. Behind me, Raðulfr is telling Marge she's an excellent alarm cat, and my mouth curves into a smile. He's interesting and good-looking, open to my religion, gets along with my cat, and kisses like a dream. I've hit the motherfucking jackpot. Pressing my palms to suddenly hot cheeks—right where his were before—I ask myself what I'm waiting for. So what if we've known each other less than two weeks? I've hooked up with guys I've known less than two minutes—and I knew a hell of a lot less about them than I do Raðulfr.

Taking a breath to center myself, I drop my hands and turn around. Raðulfr is petting Marge, a goofy little smile on his face that I know isn't there because my cat's adorable. That smile's all for me—and likely matches the one I'm wearing.

"So, uh... how hungry would you say you are?"

He turns his head toward me. "Starving."

Oh. My face must fall, because he adds, "Oh, you meant for soup. That can wait for later." His smile turns wicked, sending a delicious shiver up my spine. "I'm ravenous for something else right now."

"Me too," I say through a suddenly dry throat. I don't know why I'm nervous. It's just sex. Just because my inner romantic thinks Raðulfr might be *the one* doesn't mean I should be nervous.

I turn back to the stove and put the lid on the soup pot, then cross the kitchen and take Raðulfr's hand. "Come on. I know what will satisfy both our appetites."

He steals another kiss before letting me tug him toward the door. Halfway there, I stop and go back for Marge. "If I leave her in here, she'll go for the soup pot," I explain. Letting my cat burn herself isn't on my bingo card, ever.

"I'll close the door," he promises, following me out, and sure enough, I hear the snick of the latch catching. "Can she open doors? I know some cats can."

I shake my head as I let her down on the couch. She glares, not happy about being moved, but settles down for a nap. "No, she hasn't mastered that yet. I don't close interior doors much, so she doesn't get a lot of chances to practice." Are we seriously talking about Marge right now? I need to find a way to rekindle the mood, fast.

I pull my shirt over my head.

Raðulfr's eyes drop first to where my amethyst rests against my breastbone, then lower, widening as they take me in. I'm not ripped or anything—I'm a forty-two-year-old kindergarten teacher who prefers gardening to the gym—but I take care of myself, and Raðulfr clearly appreciates that.

He closes the distance between us. "You said something about satisfying me?"

"Right this way."

I was hoping tonight would go this way, so I changed the sheets and tidied up my bedroom. I even left a bedside lamp on, so the room looks inviting and we don't need to use the mood-killing overhead light. I'm already half-naked, so once I've closed the door to keep Marge out, I motion toward Raðulfr's chest. "You've got some catching up to do."

He doesn't need further prompting, and by the time I get my pants and socks off, he's not far behind. "Fast," I murmur, sinking to my knees as his pants drop to the floor, but deliberately looking up at him and nowhere else.

"It's amazing what a man can do with the right motivation." His eyes are locked on my face, the hunger in them so flattering... and inspiring.

I lower my gaze at last, and I'm not disappointed. His cock is a generous handful, flushed dark red and already hard, his balls drawn up tight. I lean in and bury my face in the crease of his thigh, inhaling the musky scent of him, then rubbing my cheek against the hard length of his dick.

His hands come to rest on my head, fingers twining into my hair but not grabbing.

"Are you going to tease me, then?" he asks, his voice husky.

"Hmm. Maybe." I dart my tongue out to nudge against his left ball, and he inhales sharply, so I do it again, following up with a proper lick, then suck it into my mouth. The angle is awkward, but the way his thigh muscles go rock-solid against me makes it worth repeating with the right one.

When I let it go, he draws in a shuddering breath. It releases in a rush when I wrap my lips around the head of his cock, and he says something in a language I don't recognize, the words strangled. I don't need to understand them to know they're words of tortured pleasure, and it gives me a little rush of power—and happiness.

I want to pleasure Raðulfr. To make him feel like a king, worshiped by me.

My tongue probes gently around the head of his dick, searching for the spot that finally makes his hands tighten in my hair, and when I find it, I torment it, teasing the little bundle of nerves until his breathing is ragged.

Pulling off, I grin up at him. "Having fun?"

"Your mouth should be illegal," he pants, and I laugh, then open wide and take as much of him as I can manage into my mouth, winning a yell from him.

I alternate using my tongue and lightly sucking, occasionally drawing back so cool air can sensitize his wet skin, and when his hips make an aborted thrusting motion, I know it's only rigid self-control that's stopping his orgasm.

So I relax my throat and take him as deep as I can, then whisper my fingers in a featherlight stroke over his scrotum.

Every muscle in his body locks up, and he comes, his rough cry ringing in my ears like music.

When he finally stumbles back, I wipe my mouth with the back of my hand and—

—land on the bed. Stunned, I gape at him as he crawls over me. Who knew he had that kind of strength?

Who knew I'd find it so hot?

"You're a miracle," he growls, then plunders my mouth with the kind of kiss I never thought I wanted. I was wrong.

It ends before I'm ready, but my protests dies when Raðulfr slides down my body and sucks my neglected dick into his mouth. I'm so stimulated from teasing him that it takes next to nothing before I'm seeing stars.

And then it's his turn to worship me.

I swear, I'm *bouncing* as I enter my classroom the next morning, and my mouth is stretched into the stupidest smile ever—it has been ever since I woke up tangled with Raðulfr. Not even the strange guy on my street who gave me the weirdest look as Raðulfr and I left my place could kill my smile. I offered to give Raðulfr a lift home, but he said he needed a walk to burn off his excess sex energy from this morning's mutual blowjobs. I get it—I'm so wired right now, and sure, part of that is from the incredible sex, which always gives me a boost, but the rest is giddy, goopy feelings.

If feelings could be converted to electricity, I'd never have to pay another power bill just based on this morning.

I've got half an hour to wind down a bit before my students—

"Well, well. Someone's in a very good mood for a Monday."

Er. I turn toward the doorway between the kindergarten classrooms, where Gretchen is standing with a big smirk.

"New week," I offer. "Lots to be excited about."

She laughs as she comes toward me. "You might be the most positive, chill person I know, but that would be pushing things even for you. No, all *this*"—she waves up and down toward me, encapsulating my whole being in the gesture—"is to do with that guy you've been 'kinda seeing.'"

"I can practically hear the air quotes," I say dryly.

"Thanks, it's a gift. Now spill. I want to hear everything."

I should protest, but I really want to talk to *someone* about Raðulfr. A guy deserves the chance to gush when he maybe meets *the one*.

"He came over last night for the new moon ritual—did I tell you he's pagan?"

"No, you did *not*." She makes an excited face. "That's great! You won't have to worry about whether he's going to be judgy about it."

"He's definitely not judgy about it. I already knew he wouldn't be, but he was so great—he's not Wiccan, so he had some questions, and he was interested and respectful and..." I trail off with a happy sigh. "Everything I could have hoped for."

Gretchen puts a hand over her heart. "Aww. I'm so happy for you. I can't remember the last time I saw you all ditzy with feelings like this."

"I can't remember the last time I felt it," I admit. "He's amazing."

My friend raises a brow. "And did this amazing man go home after the ritual, or did you maybe have a different kind of 'ritual'?" This time she actually does make air quotes, and a laugh escapes me at how ridiculous she is.

"Maybe we did."

I'd be worried about her squeal rupturing my eardrums, except I'm too busy being worried about whether the death grip she now has on my arm is going to leave bruises. "Yes! Yes, I knew it! Tell me every detail. Was it good? It had to be, or you wouldn't be smiling like that."

Her excitement validates mine, and I let my grin take over my face again. "It was good." I pause while she bounces on her toes, then add, "Both times."

"Twice?!" she shrieks.

"And again this morning," I confirm, and she throws her arms around me in a jumpy-dancey-hug that I enthusiastically return.

"What the heck is happening in here?" a voice asks, and we break apart as Kaelynn, who teaches second grade, walks in from the hall. "Are we having a party?"

Not for the first time, I marvel at her timing. She always seems to know when we're talking about something fun. Sure, Gretchen's not being quiet, but Kaelynn's classroom is at the other end of the hall, and Gretch wasn't *that* loud. If she was, we'd have four more teachers in here too.

"Jared's got a new man!" Gretchen declares gleefully. "One who makes him happy! Look at his face!"

Kaelynn studies me, and my cheeks get hot under her scrutiny. "We've just started seeing each other," I mumble.

"They had sex last night, and today he's all..." Gretch makes that up-and-down gesture again.

"I see it," Kaelynn says, nodding. "That's fantastic, Jared! Tell us about him. What's his name?"

"Raðulfr," I say, and Kaelynn's mouth drops open.

"Say again?" Gretchen demands. "You know I'm so bad with non-English names."

"I'm pretty sure I'm not saying it right either," I confess, then walk her through the pronunciation the way Raðulfr did for me. "I'll get better at it."

"You're doing just fine, I'm sure," Kaelynn assures me, a suppressed kind of excitement in her voice. "Come on, tell us more! What does he look like? Do you have pictures?"

I shake my head. "No pictures, but he's tall, with long dark-blond hair that's so beautiful. I swear, he's either got the world's best hair genes or he spends a fortune on hair-care. And he's got a beard—it's not long, just kind of hugs his jaw—but it's so soft and..." I bite my lip, embarrassed. "Crap, I'm gushing over his *beard*. I've got it so bad."

"You really do," Gretchen agrees. "It's awesome."

"Definitely a good look for you," Kaelynn adds. "So... what now? When are you seeing him again?"

"Wednesday night, but he said he'd call me tonight... and he's already texted me twice since I said bye forty minutes ago. I think he's into me just as much as I am him."

Kaelynn's grin is oddly jubilant. "It really sounds like he is."

CHAPTER TWELVE

Raðulfr

TWO WEEKS LATER

I CLOSE the browser tab in disgust. One hundred
suggestions for dates, and not a single one seemed right. I
suppose it's possible that I'm being picky, but shouldn't I
be? Jared's special. He deserves to feel like I'm putting in
effort.

It's not just me who's being picky, either. The life force
didn't like *any* of the suggestions on that site, not even the
ones I thought might be okay. Since Jared's the first person
in my life since Ásta died that the life force has taken an
interest in, it's probably a good idea to let it guide me.

I just wish it would actually guide me, instead of
merely disapproving of ideas. It's my turn to plan our date,
and I have zero inspiration. We've already been out for a
few nice dinners, some casual and some a little more
upmarket, been to the cinema to make out in the back row
of a movie neither of us was interested in—that was a fun
experience—and to a light show at the botanic gardens. I
wouldn't have thought they'd hold something like that at

this time of year, but Jared assures me they do it every year, taking advantage of the bare branches to create something spectacular for anyone willing to brave the cold. We drank hot chocolate and wandered through the magical exhibits holding hands. After that, he's definitely winning the date-planning *not*-contest. Because adults don't compete about things like this, and I've clearly been spending too much time with Brandt and his dragons if I'm thinking of it as a competition.

The part that annoys me the most is that I *know* inviting him to my home would make him so happy. We've stayed in at his place several times, and last weekend, I helped him do some work in his garden ahead of his spring planting plans. He's never prodded about coming to my place, but there have been a few instances where it would have been natural for me to invite him, and I haven't. The quickly hidden disappointment is a dead giveaway.

Eoin and the team are standing firm about this, though. They won't agree to stay in the butler's suite, where Jared won't see them and ask why they're in my home, until he knows and accepts that I'm not human. The "easy" solution to that would be to tell him, but I'm forbidden by law. Our relationship is still too new for me to qualify for the exemption that would allow me to tell him. Yes, I'm the King of the Elves, but that just makes it even more necessary for me to abide by the law. I set the example for all my people to follow—even the ones who make it difficult for me to enjoy leadership.

I offered to tell Jared I had a roommate, so that one of my guards could be in the penthouse with us. Eoin merely raised a brow and asked if I thought telling unnecessary extra lies now was going to make it go easier when I eventually reveal the truth. That was both a win and a loss—I didn't get my way, but Eoin conceded that Jared would learn the truth one day.

Then I pointed out that when I stay at Jared's, they're farther from me than they would be in the butler's suite, to which Eoin replied, "You have no idea how close to you we actually are." I ended the conversation at that point. It didn't seem like I was going to win, and I definitely didn't want him to tell me how close they get. Jared would recognize it if I spelled to create a privacy shield of some kind, so it's better for me to just stay ignorant.

Eventually, I'll be able to invite Jared to my penthouse. We'll sit in the garden and talk into the wee hours, then make love in my bed looking out over this glorious world that we both love. But not for our next date.

Which brings me back to my current dilemma: What are we doing on our next date?

I sigh. It's been a long time, so I might be misremembering, but dating never used to be this hard. I think it's time to ask for help again.

The life force whirls around me encouragingly.

I pick up the phone on my desk and dial.

"Reception, this is Dáithí."

"Hello, Dáithí, it's Raðulfr. Are you terribly busy at the moment?"

"Never too busy for you, sir. Especially since I need an update on that situation we discussed last month. How can I help?"

It's no wonder he has Eoin in knots. "Actually, if there's someone there who can cover for you, would you join me in my office? I'd prefer neither of us was overheard."

A drawn-in little breath tells me exactly how excited he is by the prospect of fresh secrets. "Not a problem. Give me ten minutes."

I while away the time doing actual work, and exactly ten minutes later, there's a knock. "Enter," I call.

Dáithí opens the door, talking over his shoulder. "...none of your business what I'm seeing His Majesty about, Eoin. Go back to your little schedule, and if either of us wants you to know what we're discussing, we'll tell you."

I catch a glimpse of Eoin's unimpressed face as he stands in the doorway to the security office across the hall, and I smile brightly at him as Dáithí closes the door.

"I apologize for using our meeting to bait him," he says candidly as he crosses toward me, "but he had the nerve to suggest that my clothing today is inappropriate, and I needed to take him down a peg."

Waving him toward one of the visitor chairs, I study what he's wearing. It looks fine to me. "What was his problem with it?"

Dáithí scoffs, but there's an undertone of smugness when he says, "I'm wearing sexy underwear, and he said he won't be able to get any work done remembering how it looks."

I narrow my eyes. "He needs to be brought down more than one peg for that. Make him beg."

Our sassy receptionist grins at me. "You've always been one of my favorite people, sir. Don't worry—I intend to. Now." He leans forward, expression turning serious. "What can I do for you?"

"Let me update you." I run through everything that's happened since Jared's and my second bookstore meeting, skimming over the very personal details and finishing with, "It's my turn to plan a date, and I don't know what it should be. It needs to be something that shows him I want him in every part of my life."

Dáithí, who made appropriately happy noises in all the

right places during my story, says, "Hmm, yes. You need a couple-y date."

I frown. "What?"

He's nodding to himself. "A date that longtime couples would go on. A concert, or a movie you actually want to see. The kind of date where you're together, but not necessarily focused on each other. It sends a signal that you think you've moved on from the getting-to-know-you stuff to the actual relationship stuff. That you're boyfriends." He meets my gaze. "Is that the vibe you want to give?"

I don't even have to think about it. "Yes."

"Great. Okay, so you said you've been to a movie already, and it's unlikely you'd get concert tickets for anyone good this late—is there anyone good even playing at the moment?"

"I'd need to check." Though, I haven't truly taken much interest in Earth music yet. A stubborn part of me is clinging to the music of my own people, and I can't take Jared to one of their shows—not yet.

"Sports, then," Dáithí suggests. "Something fast-paced so you don't get bored, with snacks and entertainment when there's no play."

"That sounds reasonable." And I can buy Jared a souvenir of the game—something to remember the night. "What about baseball? I like baseball." At least, I've been to two games before, and they were fun.

He shakes his head. "Too early. I like baseball too—baseball pants are a gift."

He's not wrong.

"When's your date?" he asks, pulling out his phone and tapping industriously at the screen.

I wince. "Tonight. The planning's been a lot harder than I expected."

He waves that off. "It always is. But we're too late for football, which leaves basketball with those ugly loose shorts, or hockey."

"Basketball shorts are ugly but you're okay with hockey pads?" I ask in surprise, and he looks up from his phone.

"It's all that power flying down the ice," he says dreamily. "Trust me." He looks back at his phone. "Plus, there isn't a basketball game tonight, so it's hockey or nothing."

I shrug. "Hockey it is. That's the one where they're on skates, right?" His comment about ice jogged my sports memory, such as it is.

"Yes. And they play with a *puck*, not a ball. That's important."

"Puck, not ball," I repeat. "Got it. Dáithí?"

"Hmm?" He's still tapping at his phone.

"What's a puck?"

"It's a... thing. That they hit. To score. I never really paid that much attention to that part. Maybe see if there's a hockey for beginners tutorial on YouTube."

Turning to my computer, I wake up the screen and begin the search. I'm very familiar with YouTube—all of us who migrated are. It helped us learn so much about this planet and its customs.

"Okay, I'm getting you tickets at center ice, opposite the team benches, about seven rows back. They're expensive, but you'll have a great view, and you'll get access to one of the lounges, so it'll be easier to get drinks. How does that sound?"

Completely foreign, but I'm ready to try something new... with Jared. "Good. Wait! Should I check if he even likes hockey?"

Dáithí's eyes widen. "Good idea. At least make sure he doesn't hate it."

I tap out a quick text message:

> Got an opportunity to go to the hockey tonight—does that sound okay, or should we pass?

There, that's vague enough that he won't feel obligated to say yes—or no. It's also the kind of message people send their long-term partners, like we're an established couple. I like it.

I check the time. It's recess, so he should reply soon.

"I can't hold the tickets that long," Dáithí warns. "We'll still be able to get some later, but—"

My phone chimes.

JARED:

> Sounds fun! I haven't been at all this season. Didn't even know there was a game tonight. Let's go.

"He likes hockey," I tell Dáithí, sending back a quick confirmation. "I guess I'd better learn some stuff about it."

"Sending you the tickets now," Dáithí says, and I get a notification a second later. "Start with YouTube, and I'll find some other resources for you as well," he promises. "I'll also screen your calls this afternoon so you can focus."

"Jared's really going to like you." I smile. "Now, do you want my help making Eoin suffer? He's annoying me to no end lately, so it would be a pleasure."

Dáithí laughs. "That's a kind offer, sir, but I've got it in hand. He needs to go through the stages of torture to prove his worthiness. It took him too long to realize how epic I am, and I want to know he's invested and not just in this for a fun time."

"It's almost a shame you're so good on reception," I

muse. "You'd be amazing in one of our strategic teams. If you ever want a change in career—"

"Thanks, but no," he replies, not for the first time. We've been offering him career development for decades. "The strategic teams don't get to hear as much gossip as I do."

CHAPTER THIRTEEN

Jared

I WAIT in front of the stadium, looking around for Raðulfr. He was going to pick me up from home, but called nearly two hours ago to say he'd been pulled into a late meeting and could I meet him here instead. I assured him it wasn't a problem, and he swore up and down that he'd be here on time, even if it meant mayhem. It's such a little thing, but it made me smile.

He's not late yet, so I lean against the pillar outside door three, using a clever spell Raðulfr taught me to keep myself warm, and watch the excited sports fans around me while I wait. There's not as many as I would have expected for a home game this late in the season, especially considering how well the local team is doing. There's also something odd about the crowd. I don't think I've seen anyone wearing local jerseys... or any I recognize. There are plenty of jersey-wearers, but they're all for teams I've never heard of.

On a hunch, I pull out my phone and double-check the season fixture. There's definitely not an NHL game here tonight. I bring up the website for the stadium and look for the schedule. Maybe it's an AHL or even ECHL game... though this is a big stadium for them.

Scrolling, scrolling... there it is! *Community Hockey League, Warhammers v. Glaives, 7:00 pm.*

I blink at my screen a few times. A local community league is playing in a stadium this size? Looking around again, I reassess my earlier thought that the crowd is on the small side. Sure, it won't fill the stadium, but for a couple of hobby teams, it's impressive.

Slipping my phone away, I shamelessly eavesdrop on a group of college kids who've stopped a few feet away.

"...Warhammers have been totally shit lately. It almost makes me want to switch teams," one of the bigger guys says.

A smaller, slimmer young man smirks. "You should. The Hammers have built their rep around dominating with size and strength, but everyone knows the best player on the team is Ansas, and he's half the size of his teammates."

"Yeah," someone else adds. I can't see them around the two big guys, who are both well over six feet tall and built like linebackers. "You should switch to the Glaives. Every one of their players is a precision weapon, just like the team name."

My brows shoot up. It sounds like this is going to be a heck of a game.

The guys move inside, still arguing about whether a team needs to earn fan loyalty or not, and I go back to studying the crowd. Now that I know what I'm looking for, I easily pick out the Warhammers fans in navy blue and the Glaives fans in lilac. I don't think I've ever seen a hockey team opt for such a delicate color. Normally sports teams pick bold shades, but this definitely isn't. I kind of like that.

There's a minor disturbance over toward the road, but when I look, all I see is more people in navy and lilac arriving. There are random others in different jerseys, and I make a mental note to look up this league later and check out the teams. I like the idea of supporting community sports. Maybe—

My gaze catches on Raðulfr, making his way toward me, and I grin and wave. He waves back, and... people turn to look? That's weird. I let my hand drop, not wanting to attract attention. It's probably a coincidence that the people near him turned right then.

I keep my eyes on him as he gets closer, and notice that quite a few people in the crowd say hello and nod to him. I guess he comes to these games a lot, which is even more reason for me to find out more about the league. I wish he'd mentioned sooner that he likes hockey—though I guess I never brought it up either. It's not like I'm a rabid fan, and when I'm with him, I don't bother to turn on a game, not wanting him to think my attention is divided. I love that we're moving past that now—that we're both confident enough in each other's feelings that we don't need to be dancing attention on each other.

I think we're officially at the boyfriend stage. Or whatever the age-appropriate word is for men in their forties. Actually, *is* Raðulfr in his forties like me? I assumed, but it's hard to tell based on his face. He could be anywhere from late thirties to late fifties. Not that it matters, but I should probably find out if he's got any important birthdays coming up.

One woman nods so deeply to him that it looks almost like she's bowing, and I bite my lip to stifle a laugh. I bet he's made some hefty donations to the league. Fans of smaller leagues love the people who help their teams stay solvent.

He reaches me and leans down for a kiss, which I happily return. We keep it low-key, because we've both talked about the fact that our jobs don't allow for highly visible ostentatious PDA. Our make-out session at the back of a cinema felt thrillingly naughty.

"Have you been waiting long?" he asks, and I shake my head.

"Just a few minutes. I've been enjoying the crowd."

He smiles at me in a way that makes my stomach somersault. I know that feeling will fade the longer we're together, but I hope it never completely disappears. "And staying warm, I see. That's some very neat work. I'm impressed."

Laughing, I hook my arm through his and pull him toward the door. "I learned from an expert. Do you have the tickets? I want to hit concessions and get some nachos before the puck drops."

"Mmm, nachos," he agrees, pulling out his phone and holding it out to be scanned. A few seconds later we're in, and a vendor stall catches my eye.

"This way," I say. "I want to get a Glaives jersey." I've already decided they're going to be my team.

Raðulfr raises a brow curiously but tags along. "Why the Glaives? The Warhammers are the home team." He sounds oddly proud as he announces that.

I take a second to wonder why he thinks it would matter that the Warhammers are the designated home team when both teams are local, but shrug it off. "I heard someone saying the Glaives' players are all precision weapons like the team name, and I like that idea. Plus, the color is pretty."

His laugh surrounds us as we join the line, and a few people glance over. One man does a double take, and I figure he recognizes Raðulfr. He must be seriously involved with this league.

Or maybe they recognize him from his job? Government employees are sometimes public figures. But if he was in the public eye enough for this many people to recognize him, shouldn't I?

The people in front of us move off, and I push the thought aside to ask Raðulfr about later, and get down to the serious business of buying merch.

By the time we have our nachos and are in our fantastic seats, my sweater replaced by my new jersey, the pregame entertainment is starting. I'm surprised, to be honest—I didn't expect a small local league to have pregame entertainment, and definitely not this *good*. It's cheesy, two fantasy characters—what looks like a devil and a wolfman—fighting each other with warhammers, but the music is suitably dramatic, and the smoke and lighting add to the whole ambiance.

The hammers clang together, and kudos to the sound guy, because the sound of it *vibrates* through the air.

A sharp breath beside me draws my attention to Raðulfr. He's staring at the ice, pale.

"Are you okay?" I ask, concerned. It can't be dinner disagreeing with him, because he's barely touched his nachos.

He turns a wide-eyed, slightly panicked gaze on me, and then seems to shake it off. "Yes. I'm fine. Sorry, I... uh, I remembered something for work. Do you... Would it be okay if we didn't stay?"

Shocked, I gape at him. "You want to *leave*?" I glance back at the ice in confusion, wondering what about the fake fight reminded him of work. "Do you have to cancel our date and go back to the office?"

His throat works as he swallows, and he musters a smile. "No. No, of course not. I don't know what I was thinking. It can wait until tomorrow."

All his earlier relaxation and happiness seem to be gone, but I guess if he'd worried about work... "We can go if you need to," I begin, but he shakes his head firmly.

"No. It's fine. I don't want to miss out on this time with you. Let's enjoy our date."

Not entirely convinced, I turn back to the entertainment just as the hammers strike each other again, and I swear, this time there are sparks as well as the noise. I lean toward Raðulfr. "The effects for this are incredible," I say, then drop my voice to a murmur as I add, "If I couldn't see for myself that it wasn't, I'd swear those sparks were magic, they're so realistic."

"But you can see they're not! Because they're not. You're experienced enough to know that you can see it, and if you can't, it's not magic."

I shoot him a look, not liking the forced smile on his face, but before I can ask again if he's okay, the music peaks and the fight ends, the wolfman vanquished by the devil. Raðulfr rises to his feet with the rest of the crowd, applauding, and I follow suit. It was a great performance.

The lights come back up to full as we sit again, and Raðulfr mutters something that I don't catch. It sounds like he said something about sorcery, but I must have misheard.

"So," I begin, trying to get some positive vibes back, "I guess you're going for the Warhammers?"

Raðulfr seems to pull himself together, and his smile this time is the teasing one I'm used to. "Yep! Felix Ansas is my favorite player. We're going to smash your precision Glaives."

I scoff. "You wish. We'll slip in and strike before you can even lift your overhyped weapon." I have no idea if that's actually true. Or even if what I said makes sense.

From the sideways look Raðulfr is giving me, he doesn't think so. "Overhyped weapon? You didn't think it was overhyped the other night when you were begging for it."

My jaw drops, and I sputter a laugh. "Did you just make a dick joke? You're comparing your dick to a *warhammer*?"

He winces. "Yeah, in hindsight, not my best choice. I like to think I have more finesse than that."

"Oh, you do," I assure him, though I'm still laughing. "But you're sadly mistaken if you think I'm not going to start referring to your cock as your warhammer."

His laugh joins mine, and as the players start to skate out and the announcer begins his spiel, I lean my shoulder against his, ready for a fun night. I'll never remember the players' names anyway, so I let my attention drift across the crowd. The devil from the pregame show must be the mascot, because there are a lot of people in the crowd wearing horns, and they're kind of cool.

"Did you see where they were selling the horns?" I ask Raðulfr. "I know I said I was going for the Glaives, but I think I want to buy a pair anyway. They look great, and they'd be perfect for Halloween."

"No. Um... I think they were limited edition. They don't have them here tonight."

Minor disappointment curls in my stomach. "Oh. That's a pity. I guess I'll have to be happy with my jersey."

The game starts just a few minutes later, and from the start I'm surprised by the level of play. It's not NHL-good, but *damn*, these players have a lot more skill than I was expecting to see from a community league. And they're *fast*. Way fast, super fast... "I had my eyes on that guy the whole time and didn't see him move" fast.

The kids I was eavesdropping on were right about the Warhammers being a bigger team—with the exception of Ansas, who's a *lot* smaller than I thought he would be, they're all well over six feet, and even pads wouldn't make a man look that big if he wasn't. The Glaives have some super-big players too, but the team is more of a mix of—

Crash!

The boards vibrate so hard, I'm sure the plexiglass is going to give up as one of the Warhammers shoulder-checks a Glaive with an elbow into the back of him, the hit high enough to be illegal. I wait for the ref to call the penalty, but play continues like nothing happened, the only protests coming from the Glaives supporters in the crowd.

I think this league might play rougher than I'm used to.

CHAPTER FOURTEEN
Raðulfr

THIS IS BAD. Very bad. Very *very* bad. One might even call it a disaster. While Jared is transfixed by the preternatural speed of the players he doesn't realize aren't human, I slip my phone from my pocket and hold it in my lap while I text Eoin. He's sitting in the lounge behind us, hidden by the same distortion shield he used to get into said lounge, since Dáithí selected a nosebleed-section ticket for him.

Why didn't you stop us?!

It takes only a moment for him to reply.

EOIN:

Stop you from what?

RAÐULFR:

COMING HERE! To a community event with Jared, a HUMAN WHO DOESN'T KNOW ABOUT US!

I can't believe he's playing coy right now. He might not like my relationship with Jared, but I never thought he—

EOIN:

> You didn't know? I thought you knew and had a plan! I thought you were getting back at me and the others by coming here!

I twist in my seat and look up toward where he's now standing at the top of the steps, wide-eyed shock on his face. I shake my head slightly, pulling a face, and he closes his eyes for a second.

My phone vibrates again.

EOIN:

> Can you leave? Make up an excuse?

RAÐULFR:

> Already tried that. Not happening. What kind of plan did you think I had?

Maybe I can use that. Because we're only a few minutes into the game, and already there have been a couple dozen incidents that could have given away the secret.

EOIN:

> I don't know! Something that a wise king with the connection to the life force would have thought of!

Not. Helpful.

RAÐULFR:

> We're just going to have to ride it out and hope for the best. I'll try to keep him distracted.

So much for Dáithí's idea that we were at the stage of our relationship where we could spend time together but focused on other things. I need all his attention to be on me, and not the hellhound across the aisle who's growling in a way no human ever could about the goal the Glaives just scored.

A sideways glance at Jared shows he's too busy clapping and cheering to notice. This is going to be a nail-biter of a game, but not for the reason competitive sports usually are.

He turns to me with a huge smile. "Did you see that goal? It was so fast, I missed it!"

"Me too." I sound a lot less enthusiastic than I should, but he just laughs.

"Aw, come on. Don't be sore just because your team isn't winning."

Pulling myself together, I nod. "You're right. There's plenty of time for the Warhammers to turn this around." Hopefully without doing anything too inhuman.

He gives me a quick, affectionate kiss and then goes back to watching the game, and I divide my attention between what's happening on the ice and the crowd. How did this happen? Why would Dáithí—

Shit. This is my fault. I never told Dáithí that Jared is human, and Eoin wouldn't have told him either, since he doesn't know I've been consulting his sort-of boyfriend for dating advice. When Dáithí said hockey, I assumed he meant the human league, not the Community Hockey League. And the "hockey primer" email he sent me so I could "study" for tonight only covered basic hockey terms and rules (like the puck has to go into the net to score a goal), plus a four-line summary about the team names, their colors, and the names of the most popular players on each. I know better than to enter an unknown situation without full background, but living on Earth, at peace, without the imminent threat of my whole species being destroyed, has dulled my edge.

Plus, maybe Eoin had a point that I was getting back at my security team. Not by coming here and risking exposure, but by not giving them full access to my plans ahead of time and letting them do the risk analyses I know they prefer. Just because they're trained to react to any bad situation that comes up doesn't mean I shouldn't give them whatever they need to be prepared. This whole mess—

"Is that a streaker?!" I shout as a demon two rows in front of us teleports out. He's huge like most demons, and he was standing... My heartbeat picks up pace while I wait to see if Jared noticed.

"Where?" he asks, his head swiveling left and right, and I try not to sigh with relief as I point to the top level on the opposite side of the stadium.

"Over there... no, to the left... there, do you see him?" There isn't a streaker, of course, but I must be convincing, because most of the people around us are now also looking, and I can only hope I'm not creating a problem for myself.

"I don't see him," Jared says. "Are you sure it was a streaker? Nobody seems to care, and who'd take their clothes off in an ice rink, anyway?" He's still scanning the mostly empty seats in that section, and I'm grateful for his distraction when the demon teleports back in, a can of beer in each hand. He passes one to his friend, and they both sit.

"Maybe it was just somebody wearing a beige coat," I

suggest. "I don't see them now. Sorry—I guess I overreacted." I really hope I don't have to do that again.

He pats my arm. "Don't worry about it."

We both look back at the ice just as "my favorite player," Ansas, swings his stick at the head of another player on his own team. The other guy, who's about a foot taller and wider than Ansas, goes down like a pile of bricks... amid the pieces of Ansas's broken stick. The whistle blows.

"Whoa," Jared says. "That's gonna get him ejected for sure. Suspended, too."

I wince. I may not know much about hockey, but I do know how the community plays sports.

The referee makes the call.

"Two minutes?" Jared turns wide eyes to me. "That was a *minor* penalty? He assaulted another player! His own teammate!"

I shrug. "I don't get it either," I say weakly as Ansas is dragged toward the box by four of his much bigger teammates, shouting threats and obscenities the whole way. Someone needs to remind him that these games are supposed to be family friendly.

"This is the weirdest game I've ever been to," Jared says, shaking his head as the play resumes. "So much rougher than any league I've ever seen."

"They probably weren't allowed to play in any of those," I offer, and it's the most truthful thing I've said since we arrived.

A few minutes pass without any other disasters, and I'm actually watching the game—which is better than I expected—when someone tugs my sleeve.

"Psst!"

I look right. There's an empty chair beside me, but the

woman—a vampire, I think—in the one next to that is gesturing for me to lean over. With a quick glance to make sure Jared isn't paying attention, I lean.

"What's that all about?" she whispers. "The penalty and the streaker?"

I pull a face. "He's human and doesn't know."

Her mouth drops open into a perfect O. "Why did you bring him?" she hisses.

"It was an accident!" She obviously doesn't recognize me, because it's been a long time since a stranger has castigated me. "But I can't think of a reason to leave that won't make him suspicious, so—"

She holds up a hand. "Say no more. Distraction is key. We've got you." She turns away to talk to the people on her other side, and I straighten in my seat.

"What did she want?" Jared asks softly, his eyes still on the ice.

"To ask if I have a mint," I lie. "I don't." At least that part is true.

He nods, then leaps to his feet to cheer as the Glaives steal the puck and race down the ice, thankfully not noticing the way my seat neighbor is now leaning forward to whisper to the people in front of us.

The rest of the first period passes without disaster, and the group in front of us, an incubus, a sorcerer, and a vampire, turn around to engage us in casual conversation during the intermission, keeping Jared's attention away from the rest of the crowd. I give my neighbor a grateful smile, and she winks back.

My phone vibrates.

EOIN:

How's it going?

RAÐULFR:

A few close calls. The people near us
know and are helping to run interference.

EOIN:

Can you pretend to be sick?

I consider it for a moment. Sure, I could pull it off, but it would mean another lie, and one that's likely to make Jared worry about me. I hate that idea. Plus, he's having fun. Aside from the occasional panicky moment on my part, this date is a success.

RAÐULFR:

No.

The players skate back out, and I put my phone in my pocket, ignoring the vibration as a new message arrives. Eoin's just going to have to accept my decision. I've been managing things just fine so far, and now I have help.

That help proves itself five minutes into the second period, when some dragons in the next section over send up some magical lights to celebrate the Warhammers' first goal.

"Let's start a wave!" my neighbor shouts, surging to her feet and throwing up her arms, and the people surrounding us immediately do the same, momentarily blocking our sightlines. She must have told them all while I wasn't paying attention.

Jared and I belatedly join in, though when we sit again (after having successfully started the wave), he looks toward where the dragons are sitting. "I could have sworn I saw fireworks or something," he says.

"Probably laser lights," the felid shifter behind us announces. "Kids bring them everywhere."

Jared glances over his shoulder at the man. "Good point."

"Thank you," I mouth, and get a firm nod in return.

We've made it almost to the end of the period when one of the bigger Glaives' players checks a Warhammer into the boards right in front of us. We're close enough to see the buckle on his helmet give way as the helmet pops off...

"Is he wearing *horns* under his helmet?" Jared asks incredulously.

I open my mouth to give a reason for that absurdity, but the life force isn't finished fucking with me yet. The teenagers sitting in the front row are jeering and shouting taunts, and the big demon Warhammer raises his gloved fists and slams them against the plexiglass.

It cracks.

But worse... one of the teens loses control and shifts into his hellhound form.

The men in front of us surge to their feet, trying to block Jared from seeing, but one glance at his face tells me it's too late. He scrambles to stand on his seat and look *over* the crowd, and I don't need to do the same to know what he sees.

The horned player.

The cracked plexiglass.

The hellhound teen, who may be shifting back to biped as he watches.

The hundreds of horned spectators in the crowd around us.

Put them together with the hard hits and seemingly lawless play, the not-magic from earlier, and my behavior since we got here, and there's no way he's not coming to a conclusion that's going to need a big explanation from me.

His knees seemingly give way, and he sinks down, drawing them to his chest as he looks at me with a pale face. His hand is shaking when he lifts it to run through his hair.

"Raðulfr? Was there a hallucinogen in my nachos?"

CHAPTER FIFTEEN

Jared

THERE'S a split second when he considers telling me I might have been drugged—I can see it in his face. Then he squeezes his eyes closed and shakes his head.

I don't know what upsets me more: The fuckery that's been going on without me noticing, or the fact that he's been lying to me all night and considered doing it again.

Has he been lying to me all along?

"What is this?" I whisper. I don't know what else to say. What to do. The people surrounding us have all gone oddly silent, and they're watching me. Did they all know? Oh, goddess—are they all...

What are they?

"We should go," Raðulfr says quietly. "This isn't the place to talk. I'll tell you everything, but not here."

As if to punctuate his words, the siren goes for the end of the second period. Around us, people start making their way up the stairs to go to the bathroom or visit concessions, and our odd little group that I didn't even know was a group gets a few curious looks.

"Yeah, let's get out of here." It's not like I'd be able to

enjoy the third period—and the Glaives are going to win anyway. The Warhammers might be a bigger team, but they mostly suck.

A semi-hysterical laugh escapes me. I can't believe I'm thinking about the quality of a hockey team right now.

"It's going to be okay," one of the guys from the row in front of us says earnestly, and I just gape at him. He doesn't have horns—does that mean he's a werewolf?

Goddess, is *Raðulfr* a werewolf?

"He's right," the woman on Raðulfr's other side adds. I'm pretty sure she wasn't asking for a mint earlier. "It's a shock now, but you'll see. Don't worry."

I don't know what to say, but thankfully Raðulfr handles it. Which he *should*, since he's the one who put me in this position to begin with.

"Thank you all so much for your help," he's saying, and I wonder if the god and goddess would understand if I kicked him. That's not really doing harm, is it? "If you call the DEA offices tomorrow and give the receptionist your names, he'll arrange tickets for you to the next game."

"You work for the *Drug Enforcement Administration?*" I blurt. Has he been drugging me after all? Is the government using drugs to turn people into werewolves and... whatever those horned people are?

Raðulfr sighs. "No."

"Wrong DEA, honey," the woman says, and my poor brain tries to think what else it could stand for.

"Sir?"

I look up toward the new voice. It belongs to a tall man with a serious face whose gaze is locked on Raðulfr.

"We're going," replies my... I don't know what he is anymore, and the man nods, stepping back and blocking passersby so we have room to leave the row.

I lead the way, mostly because I have no idea what else to do, but it's loud and chaotic in here, I'm surrounded by people I'm not even sure are people, and if I want answers —or even just to put this whole experience behind me and convince myself it was a crazy dream—I need to leave this place.

So I walk up the stairs and through the lounge, pushing through the crowd without my usual manners. At one point someone shouts, "Hey!" but nothing comes of it. I wonder if he just let it go or if Raðulfr intervened. I wonder if Raðulfr and the other guy are even following me. Maybe I've lost them, and now I'll never get answers. Maybe he let me go.

I don't know which pisses me off more.

When I finally step outside, I stop and take a deep breath. The cold night air stings my throat and makes my lungs ache, but in a good way. It reminds me that I'm real. That I'm awake. That whatever the fuck happened in there, the world is still the place I know it to be.

"You left your sweater," Raðulfr says, coming up beside me with said sweater over his arm. He holds it out to me, and I stare at it. If he's got that, then what am I—

The fucking jersey.

I rip it over my head and throw it on the pavement as viciously as I can. It's fabric, so it doesn't have the impact I need. I want a *crash*, damn it. I stomp on it, hard, but even that doesn't satisfy the anger in me.

I haven't been this angry for so long. Not since I rebuilt my life. And that makes me want to cry—the *jersey* makes me want to cry, because less than two hours ago, I was so happy. I was making plans to get involved in a fucking "local" hockey league, because I thought it was important to Raðulfr. That jersey stood for a new phase of my life where I was part of *his* life. The people in that stadium? People I thought were just like me, hockey fans with regular lives who wanted to get involved with a sport they loved? I was going to join their community.

Now I don't even know what they are. What he is.

Snatching the sweater from Raðulfr, I yank it on, then turn on him. "What are you?"

He glances around. There's nobody nearby except the guy who called him Sir, standing five paces away and pretending not to listen. "It's cold out here, Jared. Let's go back to your house, and I'll explain everything."

"You think I'll let you in my house?" I ask incredulously, and his whole body jerks like I've struck him. Guilt tries to rise, but I push it back down. I'm not sure how deep the lies run, but he *has* been lying to me, hiding things. I don't know what to trust anymore.

"You don't have to if you're not comfortable," he rasps. "We... we can't talk about this in public, though, and I thought you'd prefer to go to your house than mine."

It's a fresh stab at my battered sense of self. In all the time we've been together, he's never invited me to his home, even when I hinted about it. That's his right, of course, but it hurts that I'm suddenly welcome there now that my happiness is shattered.

"You got that right," I manage. "I'm not going to your house. Am I even safe alone with you?"

He sucks in a breath, and this time guilt wins. I open my mouth to apologize—

"Yeah, okay, we're done with this part of the night," the other guy says, striding forward. "Mr. Veddy, my name is Eoin, and I'm the head of Raðulfr's security team. I understand that you're pissed off and probably embarrassed right now, but if you want answers, you need to tell us where we can all go. Out here is not an option."

The apology dies in my throat. "Fuck. You." I turn and walk away.

A hissed conversation takes place behind me as I try to work out what to do. I got a rideshare here, figuring Raðulfr would be coming back to my place after. I need to find a car to take me home.

"Jared?" Footsteps chase after me, and I sigh. "Jared, please. I'll tell you everything, but—"

I turn around, then stumble back. I knew he was close, but I didn't realize he was that close.

"Please," he repeats, but it's the wrecked expression on his face that convinces me. Whatever he's guilty of, deliberately trying to hurt me isn't it.

"My house," I declare. "I'll meet you there in half an hour." That should give me time to find a car, get home, and prepare myself.

"We can drive you," he begins, but I shake my head.

"I'm not ready to get in a car with you yet, and I'm definitely not getting in a car with him." I nod past his shoulder to where the other guy—Eoin—is hovering a few feet back.

"How are you getting home, then?"

I glance around and spot the pickup zone. "Rideshare."

Raðulfr winces. "At least let us wait with you until you're in a car."

That doesn't seem unreasonable. I hate that he's not being unreasonable. Hate that he's showing concern for me. Hate that I'm so angry right now.

"Fine."

We turn in that direction, and I pull out my phone and open the app as we walk silently over. It's too early for any cars to be waiting, too early even for the arena staff who manage the lines to be out here, so we stand in silence in the cold night, just the three of us, waiting the six minutes for my driver to arrive.

"He's not welcome in my house, by the way," I announce. Partly because it's true, and partly because the need to cause trouble is riding me hard.

"He's not that bad," Raðulfr begins, but Eoin interrupts.

"That's fine." He stares me down. "I'll just wait in the same place we've been waiting every time he's visited."

My skin crawls, and I slowly turn to glare at Raðulfr. "What?"

"I'm telling Dáithí about this," he snaps at Eoin, then grimaces apologetically at me. "I have security. They... don't like it when I'm far from them. I set boundaries, but they've still been close."

There were people outside my house, watching my house, while Raðulfr and I were inside? While we were cooking together and watching TV and practicing magic? While we were *having sex*?

"How close?" I practically shout the question, and Raðulfr rushes to appease me.

"Not that close. Boundaries. But they were there."

I shudder, and then, just as my car pulls up, another thought strikes. "That woman at the bookstore on our second date," I whisper.

Raðulfr's face says it all.

"That was Niamh," Eoin says helpfully, and suddenly do no harm seems like a stupid edict to live my life by. "She likes you more now that she's seen your cat."

Eyes sliding shut, Raðulfr slowly shakes his head.

"Is that a threat?" I demand, ready to throw away over a decade of peaceful practice to defend Margie.

Eoin looks confused. "No. I'm just saying—"

"Is one of you Jared?"

We all swing around to look at the guy half out of the car in front of us, and I pull myself together.

"I am. Sorry. I'm ready."

"Half an hour?" Raðulfr asks desperately, and I nod, not willing to risk speaking right now. Instead, I get into the car and close the door.

"You okay?" my driver questions, eyeing me in the rearview mirror, and I try to remember what his name is.

"Yeah. Sorry about that."

He waits a beat, as if to see if I'm going to say anything else, then says, "Still going to the address in the app?"

"Yes, please."

"'Kay. Traffic looks good, so we should be there in fifteen."

"Thank you." I make a mental note to tip him extra, and as the car pulls out of the pickup zone, I lean back against the seat, exhausted.

My mind is spinning, but I know one thing: If I want to hear the truth, the sniping has to stop... or at least be scaled back. I have to listen. I have to come up with a list of questions that need to be answered. And boy, do I have questions.

Too bad I'm scared of what the answers might be.

Which brings me to the big question. Do I actually want to hear the truth? I have a feeling that once I do, there's no going back. Would it be easier to just lock the door and forget I ever met Raðulfr?

Or do I want to try to salvage what I thought we had between us?

CHAPTER SIXTEEN

Raðulfr

EOIN IS quiet as he drives the car toward Jared's house. The only reason we're even in the car is because I thought I'd be going back to Jared's with him tonight, and I wanted to drive us both. The car mostly stays parked in its very expensive space under the condo building, since all the elves on my security team are portal-capable, and that's how I usually travel. I did make a point of learning to drive soon after we migrated, though, so I wouldn't need to be dependent on others if I wanted to get around.

Am I really thinking about the car and driving right now?

"That didn't go well," Eoin says, finally breaking the silence, and I slide him a sideways glance.

"No. It didn't."

"I apologize for making it worse."

I resist the instinctive urge to snap at him, and let that energy out in a sigh instead. "I don't think anything could have made it better." Though it might have helped if he hadn't deliberately riled Jared. "I don't really know what to do now."

"What do you mean? You tell him the truth, like you said you would. He knows now—the law allows you to explain."

I know that. As soon as things between us became more intense, I made sure to read the exact wording of that law. And then I read it again... and again... and again. I have it memorized now. Jared found out about the community by accident—mostly—and so I, as a member of the community he knows well, have the right and responsibility to make sure he understands how imperative it is to keep the secret. In doing so, I'm free to give him any information that is available to the general community. If I don't want to be the one to have this conversation with him, I'm legally obliged to call CSG, where there's a team dedicated to this.

It's all clearly spelled out and very straightforward. Especially the part specifying that if Jared reacts badly to this information, if he refuses to keep the secret or attempts to harm me or any other community member, I must call enforcement. They also have a team dedicated to dealing with this situation, and when they're finished, Jared will have no memory of me, what happened tonight, and, most likely, his ability to use magic.

I don't want to have to do that to him. I don't want to lose him, but if he decides he's not ready for an inter-species relationship, I can learn to cope. His magic, on the other hand... I've seen firsthand how much joy it brings him to feel that connection with the world. He would still be able to practice Wicca without it, but it would take something from him that he doesn't deserve to lose.

I can only hope that things don't go that way.

Instead of telling Eoin all of that, I reply, "Yes, but what if he doesn't want me when he knows the truth?"

"He will." The reply comes fast enough to be gratifying. "You're still the same person, and he doesn't strike me as being bigoted. It shouldn't matter."

"The lies, though... What if he can't get past that?"

Eoin hesitates, then says, "Once he knows why you lied, surely he'll understand. Your reasons aren't frivolous —there are literally millions of lives at stake."

I shrug and return to staring out the windshield. "I'm sure he'll understand, but that doesn't mean he'll trust again." There are too many variables to be certain of that.

The life force swirls comfortingly around me, as if assuring me everything's going to be okay, but I know just as well as it does that every being's free will is out of its control.

Eoin turns the car onto Jared's street, and I glance at the dash clock. Two minutes to go—right on time. I wanted to drive straight here and wait on the street outside the house, but told Eoin to drive us around to kill time instead. The last thing I need to do is make Jared feel pressured or unsafe.

Turning off the engine, Eoin turns to me. "Are you ready?"

I nod, then shake my head.

"I'd offer to come and support you, but I don't think ignoring his wishes is going to make this go better."

What might have been a laugh escapes me as a huff of air. "Definitely not. I can do this." I take a deep breath and get out of the car, then force myself to maintain a steady pace as I walk up to the front door and ring the bell.

He makes me wait on the doorstep for long enough that I begin to think he might not let me in, but then finally he opens the door. He hasn't changed his clothes, hasn't made himself more comfortable, but he has added a bracelet of black stones, and there's a bowl of dried herbs on the console table where he leaves his keys. I sniff— rosemary, sage, and lavender, I think. He's talked before about the role herbs play in Wicca, and I strongly suspect that these are aimed at me.

That hurts. I don't know what this combination is supposed to do, but the fact that he feels the need to use them is painful.

"I guess you'd better come in." There's no welcome in his tone, and he looks past me to the car at the curb. "Eoin decided to stay in plain sight, did he?"

Ignoring the mocking edge, I step inside and toe off my shoes as I have so many times before. "Yes. Would you be more comfortable if someone else came to replace him?" Eoin's the one on shift, but given the circumstances, I'm sure someone else on the team wouldn't mind.

Jared scoffs. "No, thanks. Better the devil I know, right?"

Not the best start.

He closes the front door, and I follow him into the living room. For the first time in all my visits, the overhead lights are on instead of the lamps, and even though the room is still cozy and inviting, the feeling isn't as strong as usual. Of course, the inhospitable vibes emanating from Jared might have something to do with that.

"Where's Marge?" I ask, desperate for an icebreaker.

"In the kitchen."

I glance toward the kitchen and see the door is firmly shut. He doesn't trust me with his cat anymore. The hits just keep coming.

He's standing awkwardly in the middle of the room with his arms crossed defensively, so this isn't likely to get any easier. I need to just... start.

"Do you have specific questions, or do you want me t—"

"What were those people with the horns?" he blurts.

"Demons," I reply, then realize my mistake when the color immediately blanches from his face. "Not the kind you're thinking of. That's important to know—hell doesn't exist." It's only recently that I was introduced to those concepts and ideologies, and I try desperately to remember the details. I've only heard things in passing. There was no real reason for me to learn the details of human religions, especially when I know they're completely mythological.

I might not be the best person to be answering his questions, but how do I explain that without first telling him I was born in another dimension? I'd hoped to ease him in to Earth's history before dropping that information. "It might be better if I give you some general background, and then you can follow up with questions?" I make it a question so he'll know he still has control of this conversation, and he nods.

"Okay." I stop, considering where to start. "Okay. There are two planes of existence. The physical plane, where we are now, and the spiritual plane."

"Do you mean heaven?" There's a heavy dose of skepticism in his voice, and I remember that Wiccans don't believe in an afterlife.

"No, not in the sense you mean. The spiritual plane is where souls go when their lives here come to an end. They can stay there as long or as short as they like, and it's essentially an existence similar to this, only unencumbered by any physical form or being."

His eyes narrow. "And when they don't want to stay there anymore?"

I shrug. "They come back to the physical plane and a new life here."

"So... reincarnation." Stiffly, he takes a seat in the room's lone armchair. I've never seen anyone sit in it before, not even Marge. Jared prefers the plush couch.

Another message I'm being sent.

Undeterred, I sit at the end of the couch closest to him. "Yes. An eternal soul is a wonderful thing and cycles endlessly between the planes."

He gives a curt nod, and I take that as encouragement.

"Both planes—and all of existence—are made up of and connected by the life force. It's an aetheric field that—"

"Magic," he interrupts. "You're talking about magic. The energy I use when..."

"Yes. It's in every blade of grass, drop of water, molecule of air. It ties everything together." I feel like I'm on more solid ground here, since what I'm saying feeds into his religious beliefs. Except... "It's also sentient."

His brows shoot up. "What?"

"Not in the sense that it can talk"—though it's proven to have a knack for getting its message across—"but it's... it's the awareness of life." I can't think of another way to explain it.

Jared waits, so I move on.

"Because people are people and we all sometimes need to look to someone for guidance, the life force elects leaders on both planes."

"It *elects* them?"

"Invests them with power," I add. "Makes it so that their people instinctively recognize who they are and feel secure in their presence. These leaders are..." I flounder.

Eventually he's going to find out *I'm* one of the leaders selected by the life force, so what I say now might impact his decisions about our relationship.

But I promised the truth. "They're the connection between the life force and the people."

He fidgets. "That's a lot of power. What happens if one of these *leaders* lets it go to their head?"

The very thought makes me sick to my stomach. I could *never*. "The life force doesn't choose people who have the capacity to do that. But also, investiture is rarely for life. Usually a person is selected for the qualities their people need at that time, and when those needs are met, the mantle of leadership moves to the next person."

That seems to intrigue him, and I can actually see the moment he restrains his curiosity. "What does all this have to do with the *demons* I saw tonight? And the werewolves?"

"Shifters," I correct. "The background is important because it shows that demons cannot possibly be what you were taught they were. Modern humanity and religions have taken names and words and twisted them to mean things they don't."

He gives a short, bitter laugh. "Okay, that fits with my experience."

The need to hug him rises, but I doubt he'd welcome it. "Demon is one such word," I continue. "Demons aren't evil, or whatever it is that's said. They're a species just as native to this planet as humans, and most of them live similar lives. The horns, along with a denser muscle mass, allow them to travel by teleportation."

Jared's jaw drops. "Now you're fucking with me."

I shake my head. "No. You draw on the life force to do magic. Demons can't do that, but they have an innate magic of their own that expresses itself via teleportation." Suddenly, an idea comes to me. A way to maybe put him more at ease. "Would you like a demonstration?"

HIS QUESTION FILLS me with a combination of curiosity and wariness. "What does that mean?" My eyes rise to the top of his head to double-check. "You don't have horns. Are you saying you're a demon?"

"No, I'm not a demon. There's someone I know—someone who might be better at answering your questions than me—whose boyfriend is a demon. I could call him, see if they'll come over." He pauses. "Gideon—the demon—is rather... taciturn, but he's a good man. Sam is a shifter, but for most of his life he thought he was human. It was a surprise for him to learn about other species."

Wait... "How did he think he was human if he's a shifter? Did another shifter bite him and force him to transform?" I may never leave my house again. Do silver bullets actually work on shifters? Just in case one decides to make me one of them.

Raðulfr rubs his brow. "I'm doing this all wrong. Let me tell you about each of the species that are native to Earth, and then you can decide if you want to meet Sam and Gideon."

It's unlikely, but I nod.

"I've told you about demons. You also saw a shifter tonight. There are two kinds, canid—that's what you saw —and felid."

I squint, applying my very sketchy knowledge of Latin. "Dog and cat?"

"Basically. I'm not sure how much attention you were paying to what the canid looked like—"

"Big."

Raðulfr nods. "Yes. Canid shifters are much larger than the canines you're used to seeing. They're also bigger in their biped forms. They're a completely different species from canines and humans—not a mix or a transformation from one to the other. They have their own evolutionary path. So do felids. They might share traits with some big cat species, the same as they share some with humans, but ultimately, they are neither. All those movies where a werewolf bites a human and the human becomes a werewolf are just fiction."

That's a relief. "So these shifters just walk around as humans, and then sometimes they change into giant dogs and cats?"

"They live their lives just like everyone else." A tiny smile tugs one corner of his mouth. "The canids are generally very enthusiastic. They throw the best parties, and if one befriends you, it's generally forever."

Okay, that actually sounds kind of nice. I take a little breath. "So why the secrecy? If they're not evil and don't force people to become like them, why are they hiding?"

"I'm getting to that," he promises. "Quickly, let me tell you about the other species."

My brows shoot up. "There's more?"

Raðulfr nods. "The pregame show tonight? Remember

how you said if you couldn't see for yourself that it wasn't magic, you would have thought it was?"

And he got all weird about it. "Yeah."

"It was sorcery. Sorcerers are another species, very similar to humans, but where humans use magic by drawing from the life force, sorcerers have their own inner well of power to draw from, and they weave the threads of that power into spells, rather than casting them."

"Which is why I couldn't see it," I realize, wondering what other differences there are between the magic I do and what sorcerers... weave.

"The remaining two species native to Earth are vampires and incubi," Raðulfr says, adding quickly, "Remember that modern language has twisted the meanings of those words."

"So vampires don't suck blood, and incubi don't feed off sex?"

He winces. "They do, but neither needs to kill to do so. And just like shifters, they're completely separate species, so there's no changing humans into vampires."

I give myself a moment to digest that, trying not to freak out too much at the thought that the world is so different from what I believed. He makes them all sound almost ordinary, but I don't think I could ever be okay with knowing that the person walking past me in the grocery store is a vampire.

Raðulfr seems to be waiting for me to say something, but I don't know what I can say at this point. I'm still angry. I still don't have all the answers I want. I still don't know what I don't know.

So I wait.

A moment later he continues. "A long time ago, humans lived in harmony with the other species. Nothing was perfect, but there wasn't secrecy and hiding. Each species has their leader, invested by the life force, and there were two leaders to oversee the governing of all species—one for the spiritual plane, and one here. The one on the spiritual plane bears the title of god." He watches me closely, and I bet he can see when my world tilts on its axis.

"You're saying god is real?" He can't mean the god that was shoved down my throat while I was growing up. The god I believe in now, maybe—a representative of nature?

"I'm saying that the life force routinely elects a leader for the spiritual plane, and that person is the god. Here on the physical plane, the leader is called the lucifer."

I jolt. "What?"

"Those words predate modern religion," he says steadily. "You'll understand in a moment. Around nine thousand years ago, there was a clan leader who decided to begin annexing nearby territory. That happened occasionally, because people are people, but eventually this clan leader's actions got out of hand. His species leader tried to pull him into line, and when that didn't work, the lucifer stepped in and stripped the clan of all the territory it had taken, returning it to its previous owners."

If this story didn't have words like "lucifer" and "demon" in it, I'd be pretty sure of what direction it was heading, but honestly, I don't know anything anymore. "I bet the clan leader wasn't happy about that."

Raðulfr shakes his head. "No. That was the beginning of the Species Wars. The clan leader began spreading outrageous stories, feeding small discontents among all the people until old tensions and friendly rivalries turned into serious issues. Fights broke out that turned into battles, pitting species against each other indiscriminately. The rancor spread, until all of Earth was a battleground. The lucifer was hobbled, for one of the rumors spread was that the lucifer's presence on Earth was a punishment, that they had been cast out of the spiritual plane. Everyone knew it wasn't true, but others who wanted an excuse to defy the lucifer's edicts seized on it, and..." He lifts his hands helplessly.

"Cast out of the spiritual plane?" I echo. The entire mythology that Christianity is based on came from an asshole making up stories to drag someone's reputation through the mud?

"It's not true," Raðulfr assures me, and I wave him off. I already know that. "Over the next few hundred years, the belief that the lucifer was 'the devil' took root among humans. They deemed canid shifters 'hellhounds,' a nickname that has lasted to this day."

That seems weird, but it's not the most important question I have. "The war lasted *hundreds of years*? What ended it?"

"Things came to a head when humans began weaponizing magic as they never had before. The other species were forced to put aside their differences and band together in an attempt to survive, but slowly, humans were using magic to wipe them out."

"How?" I demand. "You said before that magic is the life force and that it's sentient. How could it allow one species to kill others?"

"As I understand it, deception. When you perform a small magic, what do you spell for?"

I shake my head, confused, and he adds, "Putting out the candle. What did you use your magic to do?"

"Put out the candle," I repeat sarcastically, then gasp as

I get it. "No, I used magic to move air. The candle going out was a consequence of that."

"Exactly. It was your goal, but it wasn't what you asked the life force to do."

My head spins as the implications sink in, and I put a hand over my mouth. I've spent so many years living by the edict do no harm and glorying in the beautiful power of nature that the idea of that energy being used to not only harm, but annihilate, makes me sick.

"What happened?"

"The life force realized what was being done and stepped in directly. As I've been told, the world went dark, and when the light returned, humans no longer remembered that other species existed—or that they had the ability to use magic."

"They just forgot?" No way.

"Apparently. The other species were all granted some new abilities that allowed them to glamor themselves, and since then, the community of species has hidden from humanity."

I stare at my hands, trying to make everything make sense. "You said that happened nine thousand years ago."

"More or less."

"How is it possible that humans haven't found out? We're digging up old civilizations all the time! A skull with horns or fangs would be a pretty big find."

Raðulfr shrugs. "The life force protects. There are humans who know, either by accident or—" He stops sharply.

"Or what?" I narrow my eyes. "No more secrets."

Reluctantly, he says, "Living amongst humans, it would be impossible for relationships not to form. If they reach a certain level of seriousness, permission can be sought to share the secret."

I blink at him, feeling like he just punched me in the stomach, and logic and reason flee. "So you weren't serious enough about me to ask for that permission?"

"I was—I *am*. But the law sets out a timeline, and we haven't been together long enough to meet the criteria." He looks me dead in the eye. "I had *every* intention of applying for the dispensation. I've memorized that law, and I was only waiting for the time to be right."

"What was tonight about, then? Community Hockey League... I'm guessing the words 'of species' are missing from that?"

He grimaces. "Tonight was a mistake on my part. I asked a colleague for advice on where our date should be, and forgot that he doesn't know you're human. I don't usually follow hockey as a sport, so I didn't realize this wasn't a human league until it was too late."

Rubbing my hands over my face, I wish I knew what to believe right now. What to feel. What to ask next, because somehow I know there's more to this story.

The most random question pops into my head, and I throw it out there to buy myself time to think of the next one. "Do humans have a species leader?"

Raðulfr opens his mouth, then closes it. "I... don't know. I think you must, but since you've lost your knowledge of the life force and the dual planes, you don't know who they are." He smiles sadly. "If you ever meet another human who makes you feel as though everything is right in the world, that's likely them."

My chest tightens with the loss of something I never knew I should have, and I cast around for a distraction. "So the government you work for...?"

"Not a human government," he confirms, and once again, I try to think what DEA might stand for. "Jared?"

I look at him. That handsome face that sent shivers down my spine just hours ago is solemnly earnest.

"I don't know who your species leader is, but I can introduce you to the lucifer."

Butterflies take up residence in my stomach, and I'm not sure if they're the nervous or excited kind. "You can?"

He nods. "The shifter I was talking about before, Sam? He's the current lucifer, and I know he'd be happy to help you work through all of this. I can call him, and Gideon would bring him right over. Or we can go to them."

I consider it carefully. Do I really want to meet a shifter and a demon? Someone who's called "the lucifer"? Have strangers witness the breakdown I'm pretty sure I'm heading toward? No, I don't. But on the other hand, the idea of meeting a person selected by the essence of the universe to be its mouthpiece on Earth... that would be kind of cool. Raðulfr said people feel secure in the presence of the invested leaders. This could be a way to determine whether Raðulfr is truly trying to earn back my trust. At the very least, it'll buy me some time to think.

"Call him."

CHAPTER EIGHTEEN

Raðulfr

THIS IS GOING BETTER than I'd feared, but I'm full of trepidation as I pull out my phone. So far, Jared hasn't pressed me to tell him which species I am. I'm not sure if that means he's already decided it doesn't matter because he's never going to see me again after tonight, or if he's working his way up to it... and might still decide he's never going to see me again after tonight. On the positive side, he's not hysterical and some of his animosity seems to have faded. He's still wary, but he's asking questions and is curious about the answers. That all points to not needing enforcement to wipe his memories.

"Hello?" Sam's voice in my ear gives me fresh hope. Gideon's been setting boundaries lately about calls outside work hours, and I worried that tonight might be the night Sam actually humors him and doesn't answer.

"Sam, I have a favor to ask," I begin carefully. There are so many things Jared doesn't know yet, and I don't want to accidentally blurt them now. "I've been seeing someone recently—"

"Really? Yes! I knew something was going on with you. Tell me all—"

"Sam," I interrupt, and my tone speaks volumes, and he falls silent.

"That doesn't sound good. What do you need?"

I take a breath. "Jared is human, and tonight he accidentally found out about the community."

"Shit," Sam whispers. "How's he handling it?"

Glancing at Jared, I reply, "He's shocked and has a lot of questions. We've talked about the history that led to the secret, and I wonder if, as lucifer, you could come and reassure him?"

"Of course. Gideon!" he calls, then says to me, "Where are you? Your place?"

"No, at his." Dammit, I'd forgotten this part. "Um..." I don't think Jared will be happy with me texting Gideon a photo he can use to teleport here.

"Just tell me the address," Sam offers, understanding. "I'll look up a street-view pic on Google Maps, and Gideon can use that."

My tense muscles loosen a little, and I relay the address. "Eoin is in the car out front," I add, knowing Gideon can be prickly about Sam's safety.

"That will make Gideon happier. Okay, I have the image. Gideon, is this—"

A low murmur in the background.

"Perfect. Raðulfr, ask him if he wants to see a teleport, and we can wait for you to come outside."

I lower the phone and look at Jared. "Would you like to see them teleport here? We can watch them arrive."

He bites his lip. "Yeah. Okay, sure." There's a note in his voice that makes me think he's still hoping this is all a tall tale.

"Give us a minute," I tell Sam, standing and motioning for Jared to lead the way to the front door.

As soon as we're standing on his doorstep, I say, "Okay." The call drops out, and a strangled gasp escapes Jared as Gideon and Sam appear in his tiny front garden.

For a second, I fear he's going to bolt inside and lock the door. It wouldn't keep us out—shifters can walk through any lock, and we elves have some tricks in that regard as well—but forcing our way into his home isn't going to help the situation.

And then the lucifer comes toward us, a gentle smile on his face, and says, "Hi, I'm Sam. I'm so glad to meet you."

Jared throws himself into Sam's arms, and for the first time since I walked into the stadium and realized the situation, I finally feel like everything is under control.

"I'M SO SORRY," Jared says for the third time as he ushers Sam and Gideon toward the couch. "I don't know what came over me."

"Please don't worry about it," Sam assures him. "It's completely normal. You're stressed right now, and my role as the lucifer makes me the ultimate safe space for you."

The sound that comes from Jared is half laugh, half incredulous huff. "This is surreal. I can actually sense that—that you're safe. All my instincts are humming about it. No offense, but in any other situation, if a man with horns who just *teleported* was in my living room, I'd be freaking out, but right now I feel like I could take a nap."

Sam grins, elbowing Gideon. "Did you hear that, babe? I cancel out your scary factor."

The demon's resting bitch face morphs to a genuine glower, and only the knowledge that Sam would never let him hurt an innocent human stops me from crafting a shield spell.

Jared, on the other hand, has no such certainty, and his eyes momentarily widen before the calming effect of being in the lucifer's company kicks back in. Envy stabs at me. I'm used to being the one who gives others that sense of security, and I hate that I can't do it for him.

"Jared was asking if humans have a species leader," I prompt, and Jared turns hopeful eyes on Sam.

Who shakes his head. "Yes, but there's not much I'm permitted to say on the subject, I'm afraid. I *can* tell you that they don't know about the community. I'm not sure why the magic still selects human species leaders—perhaps to maintain cosmic balance—but I think I might be the only person who knows about them, because of my role as lucifer. Has Raðulfr told you why we live in hiding and why the secret must be kept?"

Glancing uncertainly at me, Jared says, "Because humans tried to kill everyone? I-I still can't process how long it's been a secret, though, and how nobody found out."

"Wild, huh?" Sam agrees. "Part of it is the magic acting to protect us, but mostly humans just don't want to know. We've seen some incredibly convoluted reasoning get used to explain things away, and whenever somebody *does* seem to believe, they're written off as crackpots."

"Are they? What I mean is, do they know the actual truth?"

Sam shrugs. "Sometimes, yes, but not all of it. They see something—like a demon's horns, or a vampire's fangs, or a shifter—and from there, they go down a path of theories that have never, to my knowledge, included the full truth. That's where all the myths and folklore come from: Someone seeing something they don't understand and turning it into something else."

Jared nods slowly. "That makes sense. So... you really live in secret? That must be so hard."

"It was a lot harder for the generations right after the species wars," Sam says. "Their whole world changed. Nowadays it's a lot easier, and we all just live our lives. We're not hiding in caves—we just don't do some things in public." Leaning forward, he meets Jared's gaze squarely. "I need to ask you, can you keep this secret? If you can, you'll be welcomed into our community as one of us. We have human members—stepfamily, friends, spouses—and they bring so much joy to our lives."

The seconds tick by, and Jared doesn't answer, just breathes evenly, lost in thought. My tension rises again. What if he asks if there's an alternative?

"I can keep this secret," he says finally. "It... it would be bad if people found out. Some of them are hateful to other humans—learning that there are different species would only make their behavior worse." Sadness shadows him, and I wish I could be sure of my welcome if I were to go to him now.

"As a group, humans tend to be disappointing." Gideon speaks for the first time since arriving, the deep rumble of his voice making Jared jump. "But there are individuals your species can be proud of."

It's possibly the nicest thing I've heard him say to someone who isn't Sam in all the time I've known him, and from Sam's wide-eyed surprise, it's not something that happens often.

"Um... thank you." Jared blinks at him. "I'm Jared, by the way. I didn't... we didn't get introduced."

"Gideon Bailey." That seems to be all Gideon's going to say, and an awkward silence falls.

"We should introduce you to Noah." Sam breaks it, but I almost wish he hadn't. Noah's a good man, but he can be... abrasive. Impatient. Short-tempered. I don't think he'll give Jared the best impression of our community, and I want—need—him to be impressed.

"Noah?" Jared asks, and Sam nods enthusiastically.

"He's human, and he found out about us by accident too. That was over a decade ago, and he works for me now. He'd be a great person to help you get used to us all."

"Noah would?" Gideon asks, doubt heavy in his tone, but Sam ignores it.

"He's married to Andrew, who's a vampire, and he's been a huge driver of the program to—" He stops short and looks at me. "Um... how much did you discuss?"

I chuckle, and it actually feels natural. It's nice not to be the only person making blunders tonight. "Jared and I met at one of the classes to reintroduce humans to magic," I assure him. "He's Wiccan and has an excellent grasp on his power already."

Sam sighs in relief, but Jared stiffens. "Wait... what? It's a *program*?"

"Government sponsored," Sam confirms. "As I said, we have humans in our community already, and we recently decided to give those trusted members back the knowledge of their magic. Then we decided to expand the program somewhat. It's by referral only, for humans who have the ethics not to abuse that kind of power." He smiles warmly.

"I don't know what to say. Thanks again? I guess... I

mean, I wouldn't abuse that power, but it's kind of weird to think this was so much more organized than I knew."

"Yeah, I get it. Do you have any questions you can think of right now? This is probably overwhelming, but you have Raðulfr to help you learn about us, and you might be surprised to find out other people in your life are part of the community too."

From the way Jared's blinking, that hadn't occurred to him. I'm sure the next thing he asks is going to be about whether there's a secret signal or something.

"What are you?" His gaze turns to me, and so do Sam's and Gideon's.

"You hadn't got to that yet?" Sam asks, and I swallow.

"No. I... wanted to give him the history first so he'd understand why the secret was so important."

Jared's gaze darts between us. "What's going on?"

Sucking in a deep breath, I brace myself. "I told you about all the species that are native to Earth, but—"

"There are more?" He jerks back, and my heart sinks.

"Why don't I tell this part of the story?" Sam suggests, and I nod. I've made a mess of so many things tonight, and I don't want this to be another of them. "This is a very complicated part of recent history," he tells Jared. "Some of it's classified, but I'll tell you what everyone else in the community knows. Just bear with me."

"O-Okay." Jared's hands grip the armrests of his chair.

"Around the time Noah found out about us, CSG— that's the Community of Species Government—was contacted by a species from another dimension. Before the species wars, they used to be frequent visitors here on Earth, but as that situation worsened, their leaders deemed it unsafe here, and they banned travel between their world and ours."

Jared swallows hard but doesn't speak.

"Over time, especially given the chaos that our ancestors were going through, the community's memory of these people faded, so Caolan—that's the name of the scout we met—was a surprise to us all. His story was confirmed by the magic—"

"Sorry," Jared interrupts. "That's the second time you've talked about 'the magic.' What do you mean?"

"The life force," I explain quietly. "A difference in terminology."

He meets my gaze and quickly looks away, and a wave of pain flows through my being. That's not a good sign.

"Anyway, Caolan told us that due to the repeated, prolonged misuse of magic by a person who has since been executed, their dimension was collapsing. They had only months left before the planet and the species who lived there were destroyed. The lucifer before me immediately offered them sanctuary here." Sam pauses, but Jared doesn't comment.

"The dominant sentient beings from that dimension migrated to Earth and joined our community. The species are dragon shifters"—Jared gasps—"and elves."

CHAPTER NINETEEN

Jared

MY INSTINCTS ARE CALM, and that's the only thing that keeps me from thinking this is all a scam. That, and the way energy ebbs and flows from Sam. I've spent a lot of years building a connection to the world around me, to the power of nature and the god and godde—

I flinch away from that thought. I'm not ready to process it yet.

But I don't doubt that Sam is a representative of the energy that makes up the world, whether they want to call it the life force or the magic or the blessed sparkles of sky. I can feel that in every atom of my body and soul. And if he's the representative—the lucifer—then what he's telling me is true.

It's a lot.

It's also... amazing. Wonderful. Terrifying, and a huge responsibility to keep this secret, but I can't help feeling it's *right*. Like a puzzle piece I didn't know was missing... which is part of the problem. What else don't I know?

My gaze shifts to Raðulfr. Dragon shifters and elves, Sam said. Which is he?

"Elf." He answers my unspoken question. "I'm an elf."

I look back at Sam. "You said myths and folklore came from people not understanding what they saw."

"Yeah." He nods. "Fun story, the community thought folklore about elves and dragons was made up, when they were actually stories about friends that our ancestors passed down... and we accidentally changed. Because oral history isn't always reliable."

That actually *is* a fun story, and something I want to know more about. Another time, though. "Okay, so are we talking Tolkien's elves or Santa's elves, then? Who got it the most right?"

The sound that comes from Gideon's throat makes us all jump. Did he... laugh? If you'd asked me five minutes ago, I would have said he wasn't capable of it.

Sam sighs and rolls his eyes. "Ignore him. To answer your question, though..." He raises an eyebrow at Raðulfr, and I turn to him, ready for an explanation.

Instead, I watch as his face changes. From one moment to the next, it's different, the humanity of it replaced by something alien... and glowing gold? I let out a shaky breath even as the color fades. I'm glad to already be sitting as I take in the heavier forehead and eye sockets, the sharply angled cheekbones, the pointy ears. There's also a hint of *other* to his eyes and self that would be apparent even if his bone structure wasn't different. No wonder he needs to use magic to disguise himself. He's still Raðulfr, still easily recognizable as the man I know, but he's very obviously not human.

"Tolkien, then," I croak, mostly to stop myself from telling him how hot he is. I've never had alien or monster fantasies, so I can only assume this new wave of attraction is because he's revealed his true self.

He shrugs. "There are many interpretations across many human cultures. I can replace the glamor if—"

"No." The word falls out. "This is you, and you shouldn't have to hide from people who know the truth."

A range of emotions cross his face too quickly for me to read. "Thank you."

We stare at each other awkwardly for a few moments. I don't know what to say. There's so much for me to process. I understand now why he had to keep these secrets, understand that he didn't intend to hurt me... but I don't know where I want to go from here. Does it make me xenophobic if I'm not sure if I want to be in a relationship with someone who's not only from another species, but also from another freaking dimension?

"You've got a lot to think about," Sam breaks in, his voice gentle. "If you can, I suggest you take tomorrow off from work. I can set up an appointment for you with the Community Integration Agency, and they can show you some resources and give you a more in-depth orientation." He hesitates. "Would you like to meet Noah?"

Noah? Oh, the human who married a vampire. I guess it couldn't hurt. "Yeah. If he doesn't mind."

Sam smiles. "He won't mind. He might ask you for feedback on the reintroduction program, though. The list of magical tasks was something he put together."

That's a little intimidating. I'm getting better at magic, but it sounds like this guy wrote the book on it.

"Come to the CSG office at eleven tomorrow," Sam continues, reaching into the pocket of his jeans and pulling out a business card. He must see my reaction on my face, because he chuckles. "I keep some in all my pants, just in case. The address is on there, and if you go to the executive reception, Candice will take care of you."

I take the card and glance at the address. It's right in the middle of the business district, and I wonder how many people walk by their offices every day without knowing that an interspecies government is right there. "Thank you. I guess this is as good a reason as any to take a personal day." I hate the idea of not giving advance warning, but it's not like I could have foreseen this. It's not too late to text my boss tonight, anyway, which is almost more surreal than everything I've learned. How can it have been only a couple of hours since my whole worldview changed? It feels like eternity.

Sam and Gideon stand, and I get up too. The lucifer—it's going to take me some time to get used to that word—comes over to hug me. "It's going to be okay."

I manage a smile. "I know. And hey, I'm lucky, aren't I? I doubt every human who finds out gets the lucifer himself to talk them through it."

That earns me a chuckle. "Gideon would go on a rampage if I suggested it. But Raðulfr is a friend." He steps back, leaving me feeling somewhat uncomfortable with that thought. "I'll see you tomorrow."

Gideon takes Sam's hand, and they're gone. I stare blankly at the space they were occupying. "So... they don't need to be outside to do that?"

"No," Raðulfr confirms. "Teleportation needs a visual reference, but otherwise is limited only by the strength of the demon. If Gideon had known before what your living room looked like, they could have come directly inside." He's still standing beside the couch, where he's been since we came inside.

I'm not sure if I'm ready to ask him to leave, so instead I focus on what he's just told me. "I don't think I like the idea that people can just appear in my home."

"Gideon wouldn't—"

"I know. Or at least, I know Sam wouldn't, and I'm sure he wouldn't be with Gideon if he would." I hope. "But there are other demons, and you can't convince me that there isn't a percentage of the community that doesn't follow the law."

He winces. "I wouldn't even try. Most of us have our homes warded. It's effective against human home invasion too." He glances away, then back at me. "I wanted to ward this house weeks ago, but I couldn't risk you asking questions about it. You would have felt the energy of the wards every time you crossed them."

A dizzying rush of pleasure that he wanted to protect me is followed by hurt at the reminder of why he didn't. Secrets and lies. Just because I understand the why of it doesn't make the sense of betrayal go away.

"Is it something I can learn?" I'm proud of how even my voice is.

Raðulfr nods. "Yes. I would recommend hiring a sorcerer or elf to do them for you, though, at least initially. It's complicated spellwork, and doing a whole house would need some experience. Noah would be able to do it, if you get along. Or I—" He breaks off, as if recognizing that now isn't the best time for him to offer.

"I'll keep that in mind. I guess... Is there like a Craigslist for the community?" It's a joke, but he answers me seriously.

"The integration liaison can get you set up on the community web. We use the regular internet as well, but everything else is there. There are several sites for finding people to create wards." He hesitates. "Or you could ask Sam or Noah for a recommendation."

A recommendation for a sorcerer to create *wards*. That wasn't on my bingo card for this year.

His reference to CSG reminds me of something, though. "So I guess you don't work for Sam's government. What does DEA stand for?"

"The Dragon-Elf Alliance." He takes a deep breath. "I have more to tell you. It's... I'm sure tonight has been overwhelming for you, but this is likely to come up tomorrow, and I'd rather you hear it from me."

My laugh sounds foreign to my ears, and he flinches. "Sure. Why not? Let's get it all out now. Does this have something to do with why you have security?"

"Yes." Another hesitation, and then, like ripping off a Band-Aid, he blurts, "I'm the species leader for the elves."

Whoa.

Okay.

I don't know why I wasn't expecting that. I figured he had to be important, because security, but for some reason, the idea of him being the head elf didn't occur to me. "Oh." I cast around for something to say. "So the elves feel all Zen around you like I do around Sam?"

He blinks, surprised. "Uh... yes. Giving them that security is part of my job."

His job and his *life*. The underlying meaning of what he's said and what I've learned tonight sinks in. Raðulfr is responsible for all the elves. I don't know how many there are, but still, to have people depending on you like that... it's a big thing. And—

"Were you the... lucifer before you migrated here?"

"That's not— The lucifer is the title for the leader of the Earth species," he corrects. "And yes. It was my decision to send Caolan here to make contact with CSG.

Percy's offer—he was the lucifer at the time—for us to migrate was an unexpected blessing."

I bet. I can't even imagine the stress he would have been under, being responsible for all those people and knowing they were all going to die. A little more of my rancor slips away.

"What is your title, then? What do people call you?"

He shifts restlessly. "It doesn't translate into any Earth language. The word we use in English has implications that—"

"Just tell me what it is."

"King."

I sit on the end of my coffee table. "You're a *king*?"

"Not in the sense you mean. Like Sam, I'm invested by the life force to act as leader for a time. This wasn't an inherited role, and it won't necessarily last my whole life—probably won't."

"But you're King Raðulfr?" My tongue trips over the sentence.

"Yes."

"Do people call you 'Your Royal Highness' or something?"

He sinks to sit on the arm of the couch. "Your Majesty. They call me 'Your Majesty.'"

Hysteria really wants to take over right now. For some reason, the only thought in my head is that I fucked a king. Not sure why my brain has latched on to "king" instead of "elf," but hey, sanity is a funny thing.

"That's... This isn't a conversation I ever expected to have with a lover." I blink back tears, not sure what to do next.

In a determined rush of movement, he stands, takes hold of my hands, and draws me to my feet. "I wish with everything in me that things could be different between us. That you could have found out about the community before we met. That I never had to lie to you or put you through the emotions you've felt tonight. It was never my intent to make you sad or angry." He lifts my hands and kisses them, one at a time, while my head spins with his words. "My feelings for you haven't changed. I want you in my life more than I've wanted anything for a very long time—almost more than I wanted salvation for my people, as much as it shames me to admit. You have some thinking to do, and a lot to learn, but when you're ready, I'll be waiting for you. Call me anytime, day or night. If you need anything and don't want to talk to me, call the DEA offices, and Dáithí will help you. I won't pressure you, won't expect what you can't give, but I need you to be safe and well. Please grant me that."

The relief that fills me could be because he's basically promising to look after me, or could be because I don't have to make a decision about *us* tonight. Either way, it's the easiest thing in the world to say, "Yes."

CHAPTER TWENTY

Raðulfr

THE PART of me that was so happy earlier today aches fiercely as I get into the car. Eoin doesn't ask how it went, just starts the engine and pulls the ridiculous vehicle out onto the road. If I ask him to, he'll stop the car right here and take me home by portal, and that's what I want—to be home, where I can hide away and lick my wounds. Wounds that are of my own making, because I was so stubborn I refused to consult my security team. At the very least, I should have made sure Dáithí knew Jared is human. What was I trying to prove by keeping so many secrets?

"Did you update the rest of the team?" I ask, breaking into the silence, and from the corner of my eye, I see Eoin's wince.

"Yes. I'm sorry."

"Don't be sorry. I knew you had to." I brace myself for the next part. "Sam invited Jared to CSG tomorrow, to meet with someone in the integration department—and Noah. He'll be in the building. The team needs to stay away from him."

"We wouldn't hurt him," Eoin protests, shocked.

"That's not..." Dammit, I'm not doing anything right tonight. "I never thought you'd hurt him. Jared has had a lot of shocks tonight, including learning about my position in the community. He's taking time to think about things and become familiar with this new world. It will be easier for him to do so without reminders of the deceit he's been subjected to, so to that end, my security team and I will stay out of his way." I marvel at the way thousands of years of diplomatic experience have kicked in and stripped my words of any emotion. I sound like a press release instead of a man on the edge of breaking down.

Eoin says nothing for a moment, his attention on the road. "He's asked for time to think about the situation?" His tone is carefully neutral.

"I offered it, and he accepted."

That gets a scoff. "You *offered*. Self-sabotage is not attractive, Your Majesty."

Ouch. "What was the alternative? He was clearly overwhelmed, and I wasn't going to pressure him into making a decision he might regret later—or into rejecting me completely." Just saying the words out loud is painful. "Better that he has time to think about what he wants, and hopefully remember how understanding and patient I am." I hesitate, but Eoin knows almost everything about this relationship already *and* watched me fuck it all up tonight, so what's a little more soul-baring? "I told him I'd wait for him."

The head of my security team lets out a huge sigh. "If Dáithí finds out about that, I'll never convince him that we should be serious."

I'm never going to understand their relationship. "We're going to come back to that in a second," I say, because I have questions. "First, I'm sorry, but Dáithí's going to find out. I told Jared that if he needed anything, he could call the DEA and Dáithí would help him. So he has to be briefed." The resignation in Eoin's expression changes my mind about asking him to do it. "I'll talk to him in the morning."

"I'll make myself scarce until you do," he mutters, "so he can't be mad about me keeping secrets."

"Is that something he gets mad about? Because your job—"

"No, he doesn't get mad about work secrets. All I need to do is say I can't talk about it, and he's fine. He understands that my security clearance is higher than his." He grimaces. "But when he finds out that I know he knows about you and Jared, he'll be mad that I didn't talk to him about it."

I take a second to make sure I actually understand what he said. "Because you both knew about it? But you didn't know that he knew until tonight."

"Which is why I have to avoid him until you see him. If I see him first, but don't tell him what happened tonight, I'll get the cold shoulder for not talking to him about something we both know."

The solution to that is simple. "You can tell him about it, if you'd like." It won't be a hardship to *not* be the one to tell Dáithí about my current relationship angst. Whoever said talking about pain makes it better was a very different person from me.

"No. Wait... yes. No." Eoin's frustrated curse almost coaxes a smile from me. It's nice to know I'm not the only one who's got no idea how to manage his love life. "Yes. If you're sure?"

I shrug. "I may as well help you win some points, since I've got zero." Possibly I've dropped into negative numbers. "Now tell me what's going on with you and Dáithí. If you want to," I add, belatedly realizing that he might not want to talk to his boss about his personal life. I'm also his species leader, though.

"I wouldn't mind an outside perspective," he admits. "Dáithí... I think he's insecure about my feelings. I don't know. He insists that we're just dating casually, no matter how much I push for him to commit. I want to call him my boyfriend—I think of him that way, and I haven't dated anyone else since we started seeing each other, but he's being stubborn about this. He says my dating history is a red flag and he'd rather we stayed casual than set expectations I won't be able to meet."

I flinch. While it's true that Eoin's past is a who's who of sexual exploits, with nary a serious relationship to be seen, that was rather a cruel thing for Dáithí to say—and not at all like him. Dáithí is sassy, snarky, and occasionally catty, but not deliberately cruel.

"How long have you been dating now?" I'm grateful for the distraction from my own woes.

"Nearly a year. We spend almost all our free time together, but he doesn't seem to want more than that." His unhappiness with that is clear in his voice.

"Have you asked him what he would need from you to take things further?" I ask gently. Eoin and Dáithí are paired souls, so I *know* they can be happy together, but that's not something I like to volunteer unasked. Sometimes people need to find their own way, and just because their relationship would be long-lasting and happy doesn't mean they have to choose that path.

Eoin's silence is the only answer I get.

"You're afraid he might say he doesn't want to, no

matter what you do," I guess, and the pained noise Eoin makes is my confirmation.

He turns the car into the driveway of the condo building's underground parking lot and presses the button on the keyring to open the garage door. "You think I should do it."

"I think you should decide what's most important to you," I correct. "Would you rather continue like this and be fairly certain that Dáithí will stay in your life, albeit 'casually,' or is a full commitment the only outcome you can be happy with?"

He stares beyond the opening door into the garage. "Both those options include the chance that Dáithí will walk away from me."

"That's how free will works." I hesitate. "I haven't spoken to Dáithí about this, but from what you've said, it's likely he's trying to protect his heart from being broken."

"I can't change my past."

"Nobody asked you to."

I'M STILL THINKING about that when I walk into my office the next morning, far earlier than I usually arrive. I couldn't sleep, and Eoin was anxious to be here early, too, so there was no point in hanging around at the condo. Maybe if I get some work done, later I can...

No. I'm giving Jared space. I won't come up with an excuse to visit the CSG offices when he's there, in the hopes of seeing him. Just like Eoin, I can't change my past, can't change who I am, and if Jared wants to be with me, he'll make that decision in spite of the things that concern him. Me pressuring him isn't going to help any.

The quiet of an empty floor gradually gives way to the sounds of people coming in to start their day, and it's not a surprise when someone knocks on my door. My days are full of people wandering in and out.

I look up, mouth opening to bid them enter, but the door's already opening. There's only one person who does that. Sighing, I sit back in my chair. He might be one of my oldest and dearest friends, but I'm not sure if I can handle Brandt today.

Unexpectedly, he doesn't launch immediately into speech, instead closing the door and coming to sit opposite me, his face solemn, eyes searching mine. A pang of unease has me sitting upright.

"What's happened?"

"That's what I came to ask you," he says. "I had a call from Dustin almost before dawn this morning. He heard through a grapevine of about forty people that you were at a hockey game with a human last night and left before the end, after some sort of kerfuffle." His gaze remains steady. "Is there something you'd like to tell me?"

Wonderful. I suppose I shouldn't be surprised that gossip is racing through our part of the community, but I'd hoped it wouldn't. This is hardly the welcome Jared deserves. "Where do you want me to start?" It's a genuine question, because I'm so muddled this morning, I have no idea.

"You never told me you liked hockey." The accusation sits between us like the most confusing weapon to ever exist.

I blink. "I... don't. I don't know much about it." The game was fun, though, when I wasn't worrying about Jared seeing something he shouldn't. And I liked how much Jared was enjoying himself.

"So why were you there?" Brandt settles himself more comfortably in the chair. I study him.

"Are you sure that's the question you want to ask?" If I'd needed to put money on what he'd be asking, neither of the questions so far would have been on my list.

"No, I want to know about the human. But I promised Percy—"

He's interrupted by a knock, and I hold up a finger. "Just let me deal with this."

"It's Percy," he informs me.

Since Percy's supposed to be hours away at their estate and, unlike Brandt, can't fly, I really hope he's not right. "Come in," I call.

Percy enters, a sleeping toddler draped over his shoulder, and I sigh, standing. "I can't believe he dragged you here."

Brandt gets up to take Cecy and lay her down on the couch against the wall, and Percy comes around the desk to give me a hug. "There was no dragging. After I spoke to him, Sam called me. He didn't give any details, but said he thought you might need some support from Brandt and me this morning. I brought Cecy because I wasn't sure if you'd need cuddles too."

Glancing over at the sleeping dragonet, I admit to myself that it might be easier to recount this whole mess to my friends if I had the baby as a distraction. She's asleep, however, and we all learned the hard way never to wake her when she's sleeping, so I'm on my own.

I wait until we're all seated, and then launch into my story, keeping my voice low so I don't disturb naptime. Brandt opens his mouth to say something at a few points, but each time Percy gives a firm shake of the head, and he closes it again.

"...and then I left, and Eoin drove me home," I finish.

Brandt glances at his better half. "Can I speak yet?"

"Only if you're going to be helpful and supportive."

The dragon smiles. "Oh, good." He looks at me. "I'm sure you feel like this is a disaster, but it's not that bad."

I squint at him. "That was you being supportive?" It missed the mark.

"You can stop speaking now," Percy tells him, but Brandt shakes his head.

"No, listen. Your Jared was accepting of the community. When you and Sam told him everything, he was shocked, but he didn't reach for a torch and pitchfork. He wants to learn more—he's coming *here* so he can become part of the community."

"Thank you for summarizing what I just told you." I'm not sure where he's going with this, but I wish he'd hurry up so Percy can say comforting things.

"You're missing the point. People like you here. There's nobody in these offices or CSG's who doesn't hold you in the highest regard. They respect you, they like you, and they'll say good things about you. That's going to reinforce all the nice feelings he had about you before last night, which leaves us with an open-minded and accepting human who wants to be with you and will have his doubts assuaged." He leans back in his chair with a smirk. "It's not that bad. The only downside is the wait."

Is he right? I look at Percy, refusing to let hope rise without a sane opinion.

The former lucifer purses his lips. "He's got a point," he concedes, and hope *soars*. "That doesn't mean we can't help the situation along a little."

CHAPTER TWENTY-ONE

Jared

I'm practically shaking with nerves as the elevator carries me toward the offices of the Community of Species Government. The part I'm not sure about is how much of my nerves are bad ones, and how much is sheer excitement. Maybe 80/20. What will the office even look like?

The elevator stops at the right floor, doors opening, and I peer out.

It looks like any other corporate office I've been to. How disappointing.

Pull it together, Jared. Show these people the respect they deserve—they're not here to entertain you.

I'm so busy giving myself that little pep talk that the elevator doors start to close, and I lunge through them with a yelp, banging my shoulder on one and half-skidding into the lobby. Exactly the kind of first impression I want to make.

Heart pounding with embarrassment, I look around. There are two people in conversation over by the security gate that leads into the office area, and the receptionist is on the phone, but the man closest to me—

"I hate when that happens," he says sympathetically, shaking his head. "There's sensors in everything these days, right? So why can't those sensors know when I'm having thinky thoughts and need more time?"

I stare at him. "Yeah," I manage, though I'm not completely sure what I just agreed with. Elevators that can read minds, maybe? "I got distracted."

The guy nods. He's big, on the scale of those monster-sized hockey players last night—was it only last night?—but has this cheerful, happy-go-lucky vibe that balances out the sheer size of him. His accent is distinctly English, and it strikes me that if the lucifer is the top-level leader, then the community of species has a world government. I wonder how they make that work?

"Distraction is the best. All my favorite ideas came to me when I was distracted by something else," he tells me earnestly. "My boyfriend jokes that if I don't bring up a new idea during afterglow, he knows I wasn't completely focused on the sex."

I furtively glance around. Am I being pranked? Are there people waiting to jump out and yell, "Gotcha!"?

The lobby seems just the same as before, except the two people who were by the security gate are gone, and the receptionist is now typing something.

"I hope he doesn't get mad," I say politely, then wish I'd thought of something better. He already said it was a joke.

"Nah, even with only half my attention I'm better at sex than most people. I'm Alistair." He extends a hand, and I shake it automatically, glad for a reason not to have to come up with a reply to his statement.

"Jared. Uh—"

"I'm Sam's bestest bestie," he continues, and every bit

of my attention is immediately laser focused on him. "I work with him and Gideon. He said you were coming in and that you didn't know much about the community, so I decided to be your temporary bro."

"My temporary bro?" I echo, and he grins.

"Yep. I can't offer more without knowing you better, but permanent bro-hood could be on the horizon if you fit the vibe."

This conversation isn't getting any easier to navigate. "You don't know me at all," I point out. "Shouldn't you hold off even mentioning it for now?"

He shrugs his ginormous shoulders. "Probably. But I've got a good feeling about you. Okay." He turns toward the reception desk. "Let's get you a visitor badge, and then I'll give you a quick tour of the office and introduce you to people. You've got an appointment with the integration department at eleven thirty, and then we're having lunch with Noah after that. Sam said he told you about Noah?"

I nod, quickening my steps to keep up with his longer stride. "Yes. He's human too."

"Meh. I always considered him to be part gremlin. He can be vicious when he wants."

That's not the most comforting thing to hear right now.

"But he's the expert on human magic, and Sam tells me you're in the program already? Hey, Candice," he says to the receptionist before I can reply. "We need to sign in my temp-bro Jared."

The woman smiles warmly at me. She's pretty, looks to be in her early thirties, and has horns poking through her impeccably styled hair. "Hello, Jared, it's nice to meet you. I'm Candice, the executive receptionist. I've got everything ready for you."

Her calm normality is a beacon in the past five minutes of Alistair's chatter. I smile back at her, say hello, and sign where she tells me to before taking possession of a badge on a lanyard.

"Are you going to take Jared around?" she asks Alistair. "I can call one of the admin support staff to watch the phones—"

"No need," Alistair declares. "I've got this. Team Bro is vetting him for potential membership."

They are?

Candice rolls her eyes and winks at me. "I'll see you later, then, Jared. Welcome to the community."

Sam made me feel welcome last night, but this is the first time I've heard those words, and something about them lifts a weight off my chest. "Thank you."

We've taken five steps away from the desk before Alistair picks up the thread of our previous conversation. "So yeah, Sam said you're already pretty experienced with magic?"

"I guess that depends on how you define experience. I've been going to lessons—the program, I guess—for a few months, and R—" I cut myself off. That name means something here. I don't know exactly how much Sam told Alistair, but I don't want to talk about my current personal situation, and I really don't want people to think that I'm trying to claim some sort of status by mentioning him. "A friend has been helping me practice as well," I finish. "I didn't know it, but he's an elf."

"Elves are such great friends," he informs me, swiping us through the security gate. "My bro Caolan is an elf. Some of the stuff he can do with magic is *epic*. I don't think I've met an elf I disliked—their king sets a high standard for being awesome, and they all try to live by that."

"Oh," I mutter, casting around for a way to change the subject. "Um, I don't want to be rude, but is it okay to ask what species you are?"

The beaming grin he gives me is reassurance that I haven't offended him. "Sure! It's totally fine to ask as long you do it nicely like that. Most of us can tell each other apart, but humans struggle with it, at least at first. My bro Caolan says there are times he still can't always be sure if he's talking to an incubus or a vampire."

"I promise not to be rude if I ask," I assure him. I spend most of my days teaching five-year-olds how to use manners—I'm pretty sure I can handle using my own.

"I'm a hellhound," Alistair proclaims. "Uh, I mean canid shifter. Did anyone explain the name to you?"

"Only that humans used it to vilify your species and then it stuck."

"Our species leader at the time thought it was funny and made it our official species name." From the way he's chuckling, I guess he thinks it's funny too. "We don't have anything to do with hell, I promise. Mostly since hell's not real." He stops and gives me a concerned look. "You're not religious or anything, are you?"

My chest gets tight. I'm still not thinking about how what they've told me changes everything I've believed. "I'm Wiccan."

His expression clears. "That's a good one, as far as religions go. You guys don't believe in hell either, so you're not going to try to burn my house down with me in it."

My lips part in shock. "People do that?"

Alistair shrugs. "Only once. I'm over it now; it was a long time ago. Hey, Jim!"

A big horned man looks up from the desk we've stopped beside. "Hi, Al. Who's this?" He sounds friendly enough, but the expression on his face doesn't really match.

"Say hi to Jared. He found out about the community by accident, and now we're helping him get acquainted with it." He turns to me. "Jim's a demon, as you can see by the horns. Here in the office we don't worry too much about disguise glamor, but obviously outside it's a priority. Now, what I was going to say before about knowing who belongs to which species—if we're glamoured, it's going to be nearly impossible for you. Sorry, but your senses aren't developed to be able to smell us apart." He elbows me. "Get it? Smell us apart?"

My laugh is entirely involuntary, but I don't begrudge it. He's been nice; the least I can do is laugh at his jokes. "That's a good one."

"Don't encourage him," Jim says, but Alistair's moved on.

"See Anice over there? She's a cat—a felid shifter. You'll usually be able to tell someone's a shifter by the way they move. Our joints are more fluid than other species, and we have great balance. Felids are generally smaller than hellhounds, so if you see someone you think is a shifter, you can make a guess at which kind based on their size."

"Got it." None of that seems at all scientific or concrete, so I think I'll just stick to politely asking if I really feel like I need to know.

"Al, Caolan was looking for you," another big guy says as we pass more desks. Hellhound? There are no horns. "He said the glitterball tournament is back on."

Alistair stops dead. "Really? He made the spell work?" He yanks his cell from his pocket.

"Apparently the king helped him with the spell," the guy continues. "That man is so amazing. What other species leader would help with this even though he doesn't approve of glitterball, just because he knows we all really want to play?"

I try to ignore the pang in my chest. That does sound like something Raðulfr would do—like the time he helped me research how to look after kiwi plants, even though he dislikes the fruit and thinks me trying to grow one is a waste of time and space, especially in our climate. He even went so far as finding a reputable grower who'd be willing to part with some seedlings for me.

Alistair finishes his conversation and moves us along. "What's glitterball?" I ask, even though what I really want to ask is for everything he knows about Raðulfr.

"It's like paintball, but with glitter instead of paint," he explains. "The problem we were having was that the glitter wasn't giving enough pizzazz. We could get a glittery paint splatter effect, which is boring, or we could get loose glitter, but it just kind of dropped wherever when the pellet broke."

"Okay..." This is something I hope none of my students ever learn about. As a kindergarten teacher, I respect the joy glitter brings to young lives, and I even encourage its use. But I also loathe it with the fire of a thousand suns. That shit is *impossible* to get rid of. If you use glitter once, you will forevermore be finding random pieces of it in the weirdest possible places.

"What we really wanted was for the glitter to explode from the pellet and coat the person it hit. Like the effect you get from a glitter cannon, but targeted."

Oh sweet goddess, no.

"Caolan was sure he could do it with the right spell, but it seemed like he was never going to perfect it. We were really discouraged."

"But now you don't need to be," I manage. Raðulfr is a saint if he actually helped them do this—either that, or he's not anything like the man I thought I knew.

Which brings me back to the dilemma I've been avoiding since he left my house last night.

CHAPTER TWENTY-TWO

Jared

I LEAVE my meeting with Xiao Wei at the Community Integration Agency feeling a lot more in control. She's given me a ton of literature to read, answered questions I didn't know I had, and pointed me in the direction of the community web, where I'll be able to find even more information. She also set another appointment for us in a month and gave me a signup to an online forum for humans and others who are just learning about the community of species. Apparently it's not uncommon for members of other species to grow up not knowing they're not human, only to learn the hard way when their true nature asserts itself.

At least I don't have to worry about that.

One thing that completely floored me was when she explained that eventually I'd be able to slow down my own ageing and decide how long I want to live. That led to the revelation that the other species are all naturally longer-lived, and when I just stared at her in shock, she calmly advised me that she was nearly four hundred and fifty. She looks my age. That's something I'm going to need time to get my head around.

Alistair is waiting for me in the hallway, bouncing on his toes like he's at the starting line of a race. "There you are! Come on, let's go before Noah gets grumpy about waiting."

I fall into step beside him and wonder if our temporary bro-hood allows me to ask personal questions. Screw it. "How old are you?"

He gives me a sideways look. "Xiao Wei told you about our lifespans, huh? I'm one hundred and eighty... something." He frowns. "Eight, I think. I'm pretty sure. It might be nine. But I'm not a hundred and ninety yet, I know that."

"Oh." I would have guessed he was in his late twenties or early thirties.

He pats me on the shoulder as we approach the elevator. "Don't worry so much about the numbers. Enjoy every minute of your life, and don't be afraid to change things up. You said you teach kindergarten, right?"

That was something he and the others he introduced me to asked about earlier. "Yes."

"Great! So keep doing that for as long as it brings you joy, and then you can find a new career if you want to. Retirement age isn't going to come for a long time, so you can afford to spend time on things that aren't going to provide for the future." He jabs at the elevator call button. "You have the added benefit that you get to pick what your retirement age will be—Xiao Wei told you that, right? That magic-user humans can control their lifespans like elves and dragons?"

"She told me. I'd still have to learn how, and I don't

think my magic use is that advanced yet. Plus, I need to get my head around it. It's not something I ever expected."

The elevator doors open, and we wait for the people inside to get off before stepping in. Alistair presses the button for the ground-floor lobby, and as the doors close, he says, "I bet you can say that about nearly everything that's happened in the past twenty-four hours."

A laugh escapes me, and I'm pleased by how genuine it is. I'm leaving shock behind and starting to feel more like myself. "Yeah, pretty much."

"I heard you went to the hockey game last night. The Warhammers are pretty awesome, aren't they?" He changes the subject, and it's nice to talk about something mundane, even if the hockey players in question aren't human.

"The Warhammers suck. I was cheering for the Glaives."

His gasp is so shocked, I look over my shoulder to see if a serial killer with a knife has somehow appeared in the corner of the elevator. When I look back, he's clutching his chest.

"How could you? The Warhammers are our local team! It's our duty to support them even when they suck."

The elevator doors open before I can reply. It's just as well, since I think me laughing in his face would probably revoke my temporary bro-hood.

"Tell me about the team," I say instead, then glance around. "I mean... if you can." There are a lot of people in the lobby, and more outside on the street. I don't want to be the reason a nine-thousand-year-old secret gets out.

Alistair waves dismissively. "We can talk about anything we want. People who overhear will just think we're talking about a movie or book, or that we're role-playing something. It's a lot easier to keep our secret on a day-to-day basis than most people think. I just avoid anything that's too hard to explain, like shifting into my canid form with fifty people watching."

"That's not something I need to worry about doing," I say wryly as we exit the building and he guides us to the left.

"See? Easy. But back to the travesty that's you supporting the Glaives. How can you break my heart like that? I thought we were going to be bros."

"I even bought a jersey," I tease, then wince. "I threw it away when I realized... you know. I wish I hadn't, now."

He slings an arm around my shoulders. "You can get another one. They'll probably go on sale when they finish last this season."

This time, I do laugh. "With the Warhammers in the league? No way they're finishing last."

The restaurant we're going to is only a block away, and I hesitate at the door. "Am I dressed okay? This is fancier than I was expecting." I hope I've got enough left in my account to pay for my lunch.

"Pfft." Alistair pushes open the door. "It only looks fancy to stop too many passersby from coming in. It's a community restaurant, and mostly only people who know come here."

That's so cool. Sure enough, once we get past the host stand, I notice that a lot of the people at the tables aren't human. The demons are easiest to tell, because of the horns, but I also spot some fangs and claws.

The table we're led to is tucked into a corner and more private than many others, which I'm grateful for. There are two men sitting there already, one studying the menu, while the one who looks much older is juggling chunks of bread. He looks up as we reach him.

"This is Jared," Alistair announces, sliding into one of the chairs and leaving me to take the other. "Meet Noah" —he points to the younger guy, who's only just putting down his menu—"and Andrew."

Andrew smiles at me, treating me to a discreet flash of fangs. "Welcome to the community, Jared. I've been around a lot longer than these two—"

"Or dirt," Noah adds.

"—so I can answer any questions you have. Ignore my husband. He's just mad because he's only lived in two centuries."

My ass drops the remaining few inches into my seat faster than planned. I guess I need to get used to being around people who've lived in more than two centuries. It might even be fun to talk to people who were born before 1900.

Noah studies me. "You knew about the lifespan thing, right? Xiao Wei usually tells people."

"I knew. I just... haven't finished processing it yet."

He snorts. "Yeah, I hear that. I've been part of the community for more than a decade, and I still have to process sometimes."

Our server comes over to ask about drinks, and I pick up a menu. Best to decide what I want to eat before I get too distracted.

Once our order's been taken, Noah says, "Give me your phone, and I'll put my number in before I forget. I'm sorry these two idiots are here, but you can call me anytime if you need to talk." He takes my phone from my hand.

"Thank you, but I don't mind asking questions in front of them. Alistair's granted me temporary bro status."

"Poor you," Noah mutters, tapping at my phone.

"Noah doesn't understand the sacred bond that is bro-hood," Andrew informs me. "It's okay, though, because sometimes couples need time apart."

"Lots of it," Noah confirms, handing my phone back. "I texted myself, so I have your number too. Hope that's okay."

"It is." I hesitate. "I'm really grateful, but I feel like this level of personal welcome isn't something every human gets. How much... I mean, what did Sam tell you?"

There's an awkward little silence, and I look down at the cutlery in front of me. Great. A bunch of strangers know I'm a dumbass who got lied to by his boyfriend.

"Sammy would never blab personal stuff," Alistair starts, but Noah cuts in.

"He said you've been dating King Raðulfr but hadn't met the legal requirements yet for him to tell you about everything, and that you found out by accident last night. And yeah, you're right—I don't personally welcome every human who learns about the community. Neither does Sam. Alistair doesn't give tours as part of his job. We're doing that because we like the king and we think it's awesome that he's finally met someone he wants to date. Also because Sam liked you, and he has good taste—present company excepted." He gestures to Alistair and Andrew.

"I'd be offended by that, but he's not the first one to say it." Andrew meets my gaze. "Alistair and Noah might've come as a favor to Sam and Raðulfr, but I could've stayed at the office. I came because Al and everyone else you talked to this morning said nice things, and I'm nosy."

I'm still not sure how to feel about the fact that

everyone I've met in the community so far is connected to Raðulfr, but I guess I shouldn't let it stop me from learning what I can. If I never want to see them again after this, I don't have to. "Thanks. I think."

"Now that I've met you, I like you," he assures me. "I'll probably even still like you if you decide to dump the king."

I flinch. It's still so odd to hear people refer to him that way. The king. King Raðulfr. His Majesty, the King of the Elves. Would it be different if his title was something else? Something like "president" or a completely new-to-me title, like Sam's "lucifer"? Even though I know it's the equivalent of an elected position and that he won't hold the title forever, "king" has specific connotations and associations that I can't unlearn easily.

"I'm not going to talk about that," I say. "There's a lot for me to think about, and you know him personally. I don't want Ra—the k-king"—I stumble over the word—"to feel like I'm gossiping about him."

All three of them smile at me. They're nice smiles, but it's still weird.

"We weren't testing you, but if we had been, you would have passed," Noah says. "Just one thing—Xiao Wei told you about the lifespan thing. Is there anything you'd like to know about elf lifespans specifically that might factor in to all the thinking you're going to do?"

It only takes a few seconds for his meaning to sink in, and my stomach does a nervous flip. He thinks there's something about elf lifespans—about Raðulfr's lifespan—that's relevant. I swallow dryly. "I'm not sure. Xiao Wei said elves and dragons choose how long they want to live because they can self-heal, and that humans can do the same."

Noah nods. "Yeah. I hope you don't mind, but I had a quick look at the notes for where you're at in the program. It won't be long before you can do that kind of magic, too, especially now that you know you're capable of a lot more. The program is kind of rigid because we didn't want to scare people off."

That's reassuring, in a way. I'm excited to learn more about what I can do with magic—it's a definite upside to everything. "So it's not out of the question for elves to live as long as the other species? About twelve hundred years or so?" That was the average Xiao Wei told me.

Andrew and Alistair exchange glances. Noah looks at his plate and sighs.

Not good.

"Just tell me."

"Have you met any other elves?" Alistair asks. "Other than the king?"

"N— Well," I change my answer, "sort of? I briefly exchanged insults with the head of his security team. Eoin, I think."

"I'm going to ask for details on that later," Alistair promises. "But okay, how old do you think Eoin is?"

I snort. "Yesterday I would have said mid-thirties. So, I don't know... three hundred?" It's a random guess. He looks a little older than Alistair, and he's nearly two hundred.

Andrew and Alistair exchange another glance and say nothing.

"Tell me." I brace. Andrew grimaces but still says nothing.

"Cowards," Noah mutters, scowling at them. He looks me straight in the eye. "I've never asked Eoin exactly how old he is, but from things he's said, you need to be thinking thousand, not hundred."

Thousand.

Thousand?

Eoin is *thousands* of years old?

And Raðulfr is clearly older than him.

"Oh," I say faintly.

I have so much to think about.

CHAPTER TWENTY-THREE

Raðulfr

TWO WEEKS LATER

THE BUZZ of my phone against the table interrupts the report the director of finance is giving. Around the table, eyes turn toward me, and I grimace apologetically and gesture for her to continue while I grab my phone.

My intention is to put it into my pocket until the meeting is done—if it's urgent, people know to call Dáithí or Eoin next—but the name on the screen catches my attention.

Jared texted me.

I almost drop the phone in my haste to unlock it, and my hands are shaking slightly as I tap to open the message. It's been two weeks since I heard from him, two weeks of me trying to respect his space and hoping that eventually, he won't want me to do that anymore. Two weeks of forcing myself not to ask Sam or anyone at CSG if they're in contact with him and how he's doing. Two weeks of giving Dáithí hopeful glances every time I see him, just in case Jared's reached out to him for something—and getting Dáithí's regretful expression in return.

But now he's texted me. That's good. It has to be good, right? He wouldn't text me to say he wanted nothing to do with me, would he?

He might. Jared's the kind of person who believes in closure. I told him I'd wait for him, and he would never be able to live with himself if he decided it was over and left me waiting forever.

Mustering my courage, I glance at the message.

JARED:

> Could we meet up to talk? At your convenience.

Those last three words tease a smile from me. They're so *Jared*. I wonder if I'll get the chance to show him that my convenience is whenever he wants.

RAÐULFR:

> Yes. Tonight? Anywhere you want.

His reply comes quickly enough that his phone must have been still in his hand, and I glance at the time. His students are on their lunch break.

JARED:

> Your place?

That feels like a test, but I no longer have anything to hide from him.

RAÐULFR:

> Yes.

I follow it up with the address.

JARED:

I'll be there at seven thirty.

There are a million things I want to say, but I merely send an acknowledgment of the time, then slip my phone into my pocket, forcing myself to look like I'm listening to the state of the DEA's finances. They're excellent, which is just as well, since I'm not actually listening at all.

He wants to talk. That's good... or maybe not. Maybe this is part of his "give people closure" mentality. He has excellent manners, so maybe he doesn't want to officially break up with me via text message. Instead, he'll come to my home and smash my heart there.

"I knew you weren't paying attention!"

The voice cuts through the cycle of negative thoughts and faint hope cycling through my head, and a second later, Brandt's body lands in the chair beside mine. Startled, I glance around the now-empty room.

"Where did everyone go?"

"The meeting's over," Brandt says dryly. "Don't worry, you made some suitable comments to wrap things up. I don't think anyone else noticed you were sleepwalking through them."

"I noticed," Ari mutters from behind us. I twist around to stare at him.

"What are you doing here?" I don't need security in a meeting here at the DEA, surrounded only by elves and dragons who've been vetted at the highest level, aka by Steffen, the paranoid conspiracy theorist.

"Your heart rate spiked about half an hour ago. Eoin sent me, just in case."

My... what? I narrow my eyes. "You monitor my heart rate?" How did I not know that?

Ari shrugs. "Of course. It's a small spell—you've been wearing it for thousands of years. A spike in heart rate can be an indicator of fear, so it works as a panic button of sorts."

Brandt's cackling with laughter, but he shouldn't be. If my security thought of this, it's guaranteed that Steffen did too. To Ari, I say, "Increased heart rate can mean a lot of things besides fear." The last time my heartbeat sped up, Jared and I wouldn't have appreciated an interruption.

Nodding, Ari says, "That's why context matters. There's no reason for your heart rate to go up in the quarterly finance review meeting, so here I am."

He makes it sounds very logical and reasonable, but Eoin and I are going to have a very blunt conversation about this—and the fact that I didn't know. That's embarrassing. I've been wearing someone else's spell all this time and didn't even notice. To be fair, it would have been cast by an expert with the intent of remaining hidden, but still.

"Well, you can report back to Eoin that I'm fine." I don't bother to hide how disgruntled I am, but that doesn't faze him.

"I already did, the moment I saw you. I've been hanging around because I'm curious to know what got your heart racing in a finance meeting. The part I walked in on was so boring, we could have used it as a weapon against insomnia."

That makes Brandt laugh again. "We really could. Do you remember the time—"

"Yes." I cut him off, but I'm smirking. "Tadhg was sleeping with his eyes open," I explain to Ari. "It was hard to tell, because everyone had the same glazed look in their eyes, but then he started snoring. These finance meetings get wild sometimes."

"Wild?" My bodyguard shakes his head. "We need to get you la—" His eyes widen, and he snaps his mouth shut so hard, there's an audible click. "I mean... Sir..."

Aaaaand I'm right back in the cycle of negative thoughts. I *was* getting laid, which is what Ari was about to suggest, and now I'm not.

"So," Brandt says, breaking the awkward silence, "what was so fascinating on your phone? You zoned out right after it buzzed."

"Jared." My tone is blank. "Jared messaged me."

"That's great!" Brandt's face lights up, and then caution creeps through his expression as he studies me. "Isn't it?"

"He didn't end things, did he?" Ari demands hotly. "Of all the xenophobic—"

"He's coming over tonight to talk."

They exchange a glance. "That's a good thing, Raðulfr," Brandt encourages. "He hasn't just blown you off."

I stare glumly at the tabletop. "Maybe. He could be too polite to do it over the phone."

"Do people do that?" Brandt turns to Ari. "I've been with Percy for years, and we didn't really do the dating thing." I snort, because that's an understatement. He went from zero to committed with Percy in two days, no date necessary. He ignores me and continues, "If couples fight and then don't talk for two weeks, do they meet up to end things? Or is it just a given?"

"A given?" My heart starts to race. "What if he thinks we're already broken up and tonight he's just bringing my books back?"

"You lent him books? That really is love," Brandt mutters.

Ari holds out his hand. "Show me the messages. Did he say he was bringing your stuff?"

I hand over my phone. Technically, the security team already has access to everything on it, anyway. "No, but—"

"Are you overthinking?" Brandt's delighted grin makes me regret millennia of friendship. "You are, aren't you? I don't want to mock your pain, but this is amazing. I've waited so very long to see you this wrapped up in another person again."

Percy would understand if I slapped his man. "You might be about to see me recovering from heartbreak again." Those dark years after I lost Ásta weren't fun for anyone around me.

He says nothing, but the quality of his silence has me looking up. There's a soft smile on his face. "If you feel for him what you felt before, I can't believe that he doesn't return the sentiment. You love thoroughly and completely. He won't give that up easily."

I swallow. Fucking dragons. Just when you're ready to wash your hands of the lot of them, they show you what wisdom truly is.

"He's right," Ari breaks in. "These messages all look like a good thing to me. He's still pissy, maybe, but I guess he's allowed to be."

Hope takes a stronger foothold on my shifting emotions. "So you think he wants to make up? Should I grovel?"

Ari looks a little ill at the thought. "The king of the elves doesn't grovel. I'm not going to tell Eoin you said that."

"You might have to grovel," Brandt tells me, and Ari groans. "What? Trust me, Ari, when it comes to keeping their partners happy, leaders grovel. Groveling when you've done something wrong is a vital part of a healthy relationship."

I point at my dragon friend. "What he said."

"I don't think he'll make you grovel, anyway," Ari insists. "I might not have spoken directly to him, but I spent enough time overhearing what he's said to know him pretty well. Now that he's accepted everything, he probably thinks it's noble that you kept the secret from him." He sounds like he's not sure if that's admirable or worthy of scorn.

"I can only hope."

AFTER A FRENZY of cleaning spells and pillow plumping—because the throw pillows on the sofa would *not* look right no matter what I did—I look around my condo and wonder if Jared will like it.

"Are you done yet?" Eoin asks. He's leaning against the doorframe to the butler's suite, where he's promised to stay while Jared's here. Apparently my security team was all set to hold a thumb wrestling tournament to decide who got tonight's duty, until I reminded them that it wasn't the best time for Jared to meet anyone new. Which left Eoin as the only possible candidate. He wasn't happy about it.

"I don't know. Maybe—"

The peal of the doorbell cuts me off. I told the doorman that I was expecting a guest and to send him right up, so Jared is literally standing only a few yards away right now. I should have told the doorman to buzz when he was on his way up and given myself some warning.

"Are you going to get that, or leave hi—"

I'm at the door before Eoin can finish. One deep breath, and I open it.

Jared's face is just as beautiful now as it was two weeks ago—maybe more, since it's not angry or disgusted. His tentative expression echoes how I feel.

"Hi," I manage. "Um. It's good to see you."

His lips curve slightly in a tiny smile. "Yeah. You look… good. Um. I mean—"

"You look good too. Really good."

We stare at each other some more.

"As scintillating as this conversation is, I can't disappear until Raðulfr is inside the wards with the door closed, so could you maybe make that happen?"

I close my eyes. Eoin's timing leaves much to be desired.

To my surprise, when I peek at Jared's face, he's smiling. He catches my gaze and rolls his eyes, then gestures for me to step back. "Come on. Invite me in so we can ditch him."

Hope roars to life more strongly than I've felt in weeks. That definitely doesn't sound like he's planning to end things face-to-face.

I move out of the doorway. "Please come in and be welcome." The words are a trigger for the wards that he's an invited guest, and they take his measure as he crosses the threshold—with a slight shiver.

"Whoa. What— Was that your wards? The ones at CSG don't feel like that." He turns back to study the doorway, squinting. "Hey, I can *see* these… kind of."

I close the door, which seals the wards and "locks" the condo much more thoroughly than any mechanical lock could. "The ones at CSG were woven by sorcerers," I explain. "I cast these myself." I hesitate. "Has anyone explained the difference between what sorcerers and elves do—and humans?"

He shrugs, his gaze now flitting around the spacious living room. "A little. I know that sorcerers draw their power from within themselves, and humans borrow from existential magic. That's why I can't really see sorcerer weaves the way I see human magic."

"What elves do is a combination of the two. We draw from within *and* borrow from existence." I haven't moved away from the door yet.

Jared turns to look at me. "Is that why I could see parts of your spellwork, but not all?"

"Yes. I lied about that too, all those times I implied that my experience somehow made the craft harder to see."

He sighs, and toes out of his shoes, bending to line them up neatly against the wall. "Yeah, you did. But it's not like you could have said, 'You can't see my whole spell because I'm an elf and use different magic.'"

The words, though not combative, drop between us like boulders from a trebuchet.

"Well, I think you've both got this from here," Eoin announces. "You know where to find me if you need anything, sir." He beats a hasty retreat into the butler's suite and closes the door firmly behind him.

Leaving me to face my future... whatever it may be.

CHAPTER TWENTY-FOUR

Jared

I STARE, somewhat distrustfully, at the door Eoin disappeared behind. The last couple of weeks might have helped me accept that he was only doing his job, but I still don't like him that much. Or at all. I haven't decided yet.

"Is that a broom closet or something?" I ask Raðulfr, only half joking.

He looks blank for a second, then chuckles. "Oh—no. It's a studio for a housekeeper. It has its own kitchenette and bathroom. My bodyguards use it while they're on overnight shifts, to give us all a bit more privacy." He grimaces. "I'm probably not selling this whole situation very well."

With a start, I realize he's nervous. Worried, even. Does he think...?

"Raðulfr, I didn't come here to yell at you or anything."

He licks his bottom lip, and I try not to watch the movement of his tongue. We need to talk before I can jump him.

"You didn't?"

I shake my head. "No. I think we have a lot to talk

about still, but I'm... I'm not angry. I understand why you had to keep the secrets you kept."

He takes a shaky breath. "So you're not planning to end things?"

My mouth drops open. "No!" Is that what he thought? "I swear I'm not. If I'd wanted to end things, I wouldn't have waited this long. I—" Suddenly, I feel like a monster for not reaching out sooner. There was a lot for me to think about and learn, and I genuinely needed to work out how I could fit into the life of a man who leads a government. I thought it was better if we both had space while I did that, but maybe I was just being cruel. "I'm sorry. You said you'd wait, and I figured you knew that by agreeing to that, I was just taking the time I needed."

The grin that takes over his face is wide and gorgeous. He closes the distance between us in three fast steps, reaching for me—then lets his arms drop uncertainly, as though he's not sure if a hug would be welcome.

Screw that bullshit.

I yank him into a hug, burying my face in the side of his neck, and his arms come around me so tight that my breathing is restricted. Doesn't matter. I've got enough air to be able to take in the scent of him, and something inside me unknots. I didn't know exactly how much I missed him until this moment, having him in my arms again.

"You're here," he murmurs, and I nod against his skin.

"I'm here. And I'm not going anywhere." I pull back slightly, ignoring his wordless protest. I need to see his face right now. "If that's okay with you?"

"If you want to be here, I'm never letting you go," he promises, and the last of my stress drops away.

"Okay. Good. Is... um, is there somewhere we can sit? I

want… Well, I want a lot of things, but I think we need to talk first."

The wicked smile that curves his mouth sends tingles through my whole body. "We could go up to the den. It opens into my garden." He leans in to brush a soft kiss on my lips, and whispers, "And my bedroom is right next door."

Heat flashes through me. "Perfect," I croak. I still can't believe how easy it is for him to turn me on. I've always had a healthy sex drive, but this is kind of ridiculous. Amazing, but ridiculous.

I hope it never changes.

Raðulfr leads me across the room and up the stairs, and I take advantage of the moments to look around his condo. Maybe later I'll ask for a proper tour. It's nice, but somehow it doesn't scream "Raðulfr" to me.

At the top of the stairs, we turn left to go through a doorway. He flips a light switch, and as lamps go on around the room and warm floodlights flick to life outside, I see where he actually lives.

"This is lovely." I mean it. The walls and ceiling are painted a deep, inviting green, and there are plush chairs and a sofa pointed toward a cozy gas fireplace. It doesn't rival the big wood-burning one downstairs, but somehow, this is nicer. The rug underfoot is soft, and the walls and furniture are crowded with paintings, photos, and assorted bric-a-brac that should make the room feel cluttered, but don't. Maybe because none of it is there "to decorate." It all looks like stuff Raðulfr genuinely wants in his personal space.

"This is home now." There's an edge of sadness to the words, reminding me that he was forced to leave his home-world and can never go back.

Through the french doors, the garden beckons, but I resist. It's a chilly night, and we have too much ground to cover already. Exploring outside can wait for another time.

"Can I get you a drink?" Raðulfr offers. "Or a snack?"

I shake my head and turn away from the window, going to sit on the sofa. "No, thanks. Sit with me."

He's beside me almost before I've finished getting the sentence out, and my confidence plumps up. I'm sorry to have made him unhappy, but it's nice knowing I've been missed. At one point in the mess of trying to untangle my feelings, I wondered if he'd even noticed my absence.

"I've learned a lot lately," I begin carefully, "and there's still so much more I don't know."

Raðulfr nods. "That's true, and I'm not trying to detract from this specific situation, but one thing you grow to accept over time is that it's impossible to know everything. I've been alive a long time, and there are things I'll never know."

"Yes." I seize on the opening. "I've always been willing to accept that, but I'd like to understand as much as possible about the community I'm living in. Especially if I'm going to be a bigger part of that community going forward..." I let the words hang between us, wondering if he'll understand what I'm implying.

His face doesn't change. It's attentive and eager, but nothing else. I'm going to have to be more explicit.

"Last time we spoke, I was angry," I start, choosing my words carefully, and he jumps in.

"You were entitled to be. You had a lot of shocks, and you found out I'd been lying... I would have been surprised if you weren't angry."

"Thank you. I appreciate that. I want to be clear, though, that I'm not angry anymore, and I don't hold a grudge about the lies. You were protecting a whole society, and there wasn't any other choice. I... I don't love that we started out with so many secrets and mistruths, but I understand why it had to be that way." I'll always be unhappy about what went down. There's no way to change the feeling that I was duped. But Raðulfr wouldn't be the man he is if he was capable of betraying his people's safety for his own best interests. He wouldn't be the man I fell for. So I'm going to have to move on from that and embrace the truth I'm now a part of.

The anguish on his face goes a long way toward reassuring me of his good intentions. "If I could have told you—"

"I know. Now that I've had time to think things through, I know you would have told me if you could have. I respect that you didn't. You've seen your people through horrors I can't even imagine, and I respect the way you continue to protect them."

He swallows hard, his eyes momentarily glassy. "Thank you. But I want to be clear that I was ready to tell you as soon as the law allowed. We might not have known each other that long, but I knew... Well, I knew how I felt. Feel. And I was certain I could trust you not to betray us."

Warmth slithers through me, and unable to resist, I lean forward and gently kiss him, pulling back before either of us can get carried away.

His chest rises as he inhales deeply. "Don't do that again until you're ready for more," he warns, and I chuckle.

"Noted. Um... is it okay... Would you..."

He meets my gaze solidly. "You can ask me anything, Jared."

"Can I see you without the glamor?" I blurt. "Only, I've been told most people don't use it when they're home, and

I... I don't want you to be uncomfortable... around... me." Even as I speak, his true features are revealed—along with the same momentary golden glow I saw last time. "Oh, wow," I whisper, then wince. "Sorry. I didn't mean to sound... It's just, last time I was still overwhelmed by everything, and I *saw*, but I didn't..." I trail off. None of my words are helping this situation.

"It might be best for us both if we agree to only be honest with each other from now on," he says solemnly. "Would you like me to use the glamor? I won't be offended."

"No! No, that's not what I meant. You're attractive with or without it. I..." I bite my lip. "I don't know how to say this without it seeming xenophobic, but I agree that we should be honest. I guess I was just surprised by how attractive I find you without the glamor." I brace for his reaction and hope I haven't hurt him.

To my surprise—and I think his—he laughs. "That's not what I expected you to say. I'm glad you're still attracted to me."

Whew. "So... I haven't offended you?"

Raðulfr shakes his head. "No. I've never been in this position before, but you never thought there would be a reality where you dated someone nonhuman. It's normal for you to need to adjust your thinking."

I slide my hands under my thighs to keep myself from lunging for him. How did I get lucky enough to meet a man who checks so many of the boxes on my list? Kind, responsible, handsome, intelligent, understanding... So far, the only one he doesn't check is "human," and honestly, that was never *on* the list.

"This is good," I say instead of crawling into his lap and exploring every curve and angle of his face with my mouth.

"We both understand where the other is coming from, we agree to be honest, and we're still hot for each other." Heat explodes in my cheeks. "Uh. I was going to phrase that differently."

"It's accurate." He shrugs. "You probably have more questions."

"A lot," I agree. "But most of them I can get the answers to as life goes along." Like what that golden glow was. His magic? But why have I never seen it before? "The, uh, the most important one is where we see *us* going from here."

A concerned frown tugs at his mouth. "What do you mean? You said you didn't want to break up. And *I* definitely don't want to."

"I'm glad to hear that. But what does us being together look like? You're the species leader for I don't even know how many people. You have a security team and responsibilities. I'm guessing that impulsive long weekends at the beach are probably not something you can do."

He winces. "It's not out of the question... if I don't already have commitments, and if we let the team know ahead of time. Which makes it not impulsive."

I nod. "Right. That's okay, by the way. I get that there are people counting on you. The magic, or the life force, or whatever you want to call it picked you for a reason, and since it hasn't picked anyone else yet, that means you're still what your people need. I'm just not sure how I fit in with that." I wince. My intention wasn't to sound as pathetic as that.

Raðulfr is silent for a long moment. "I hadn't thought about it," he admits finally. "Not specific to you, anyway. I was just so excited to be with you, to spend every second I could get free in your presence, that I didn't think about what our relationship would be like when we could be open about it." He gets up, startling me, and crosses to a sideboard and opens one of the drawers. When he comes back, he's holding a notepad and pen, and he sits closer to me than before, his leg pressed all up against the side of mine.

"Let's do this the sensible way. No more secrets; only honesty. You tell me what you want, and I'll do the same, and we'll work out what's going to be best for us both."

CHAPTER TWENTY-FIVE

Raðulfr

I TRY NOT to hold my breath while I wait for Jared's reply. The smile that spreads slowly across his face is exactly what I wanted to see.

"That's a great idea. We'll also talk about limitations, won't we? Things you can't do right now because of your job, but that might be on the table for later? And vice versa."

The way he so clearly understands my situation makes me a little dizzy. All the fear that was swamping me earlier is gone, replaced by a low-key buzz of excitement. I don't know yet how things are going to work out for us, but the fact that Jared wants it to makes me so wildly happy in a way I haven't been since Ásta died. Before, even—those last years we were together were plagued by the anomalies. Now, my people are safe *and* I have someone to love. I'm giddy with joy.

"The first limitation is my security team," I say, writing that down. "I'm sorry, but we're stuck with them."

"Hmm." Jared's brows draw together while he thinks about that. "We're better off spending more time here, then. There's not a lot of room at my place for them to hang around, and it's not fair to make them sit outside like they have been. Even if I do kind of like the idea of Eoin being uncomfortable," he adds with a chuckle.

I snort. "You're not the only person to like that. You'll have to meet Dáithí. He and Eoin are sort of dating, and he lives to drive Eoin nuts."

"I like him already." He leans against me. "I guess I should meet the rest of the security team too. Do they all hate me as much as Niamh and Eoin?"

"None of them hate you," I insist. "They were worried that I was being impulsive, and they didn't like the secrecy and risks, but I've been told they all like you, personally. Just not the situation. Ari—he was there when we first met—Ari thinks you'll be good for me."

"I'm glad to hear that. Not so glad that you were taking risks."

"To be with you! I—"

His laugh cuts me off. He's teasing me, and I love it.

"Maybe I can convert the attic at my place into a space for your guards," he muses. "Not that it isn't nice here, but there'll be times I'll want to be at home, and it would be nice if you could still come over."

"We can look into that. There's no rush, though. They've all been crafting spells for warmth and comfort for a long time, and it's practically second nature now."

"A long time, huh?"

I glance sideways at his thoughtful expression. "Yes."

"Longer than I've been alive?"

Ah. That's where this is going. I lay the notepad and pen in my lap. "All but one have been doing it for longer than recorded human history."

He blows out a breath, staring straight ahead. "Wow. That's... a long time."

I nudge him with my shoulder. "Ask me, Jared."

Biting his lip, he shakes his head, then says very fast, "How old are you?"

Steadily, I reply, "In Earth years, almost nineteen thousand."

His whole body jerks, then goes very still. "That's... I don't even know how to get my head around that number."

I should have planned better for this conversation. "Is it a problem for you?"

"No. Maybe. No, it's not. Hearing the exact number was a shock," he admits. "It's a lot. But I've already thought about this. Noah and the others said I should be thinking 'thousand' for your age, and I asked myself if I could handle being with a guy who was a thousand years old."

I'm a lot older than that, but I don't think now is the time to point that out. "And you decided you could?"

"Yeah. It's not like if I was dating an eighty-year-old human, who was entering into the late stage of their life. You choose your mortality, the same as I will when I learn how."

My heart sings at the news that he's already planning to prolong his life.

"Sure, you've got a lot more experience than me, and you've seen a lot more, but that doesn't always have to be specific to age. I'm not an immature kid. I understand what I want from my life. I've been in relationships and know how interpersonal stuff works. I don't think you being older than me is going to be a dominant part of our relationship."

"I certainly don't plan to make it one," I agree.

"Just one thing—no, two things."

"As many things as you like." I'd give him anything he wanted to see that smile flash at me.

"Did you ever come to Earth before the species wars?"

That's an easy one. "Yes, often. We enjoyed visiting here. I didn't get to spend much time here after I was invested, but before then, it was our favorite vacation spot."

"That leads into my next question—though I'm going to ask about a million later about what Earth was like back then."

"Anything, anytime," I promise.

"The 'we' you mentioned—was that a long-term partner? Because I can't imagine you've lived nineteen thousand years without being in a serious relationship."

That's a question I should have expected, but I didn't. I'm not sure why, but I'm unprepared to answer it.

He deserves something, though—and I won't ever deny how important Ásta was to me.

"Yes," I say finally. "Ásta and I were married for five thousand years, and together for a thousand years before that. We both loved coming here, and in the two thousand or so years that we were together before I was invested, we came often. At one point I think we were visiting once a year. She was always so delighted by the fact that grass is green here."

Jared does a double take. "What other color— That's not important right now." I can see that he's mentally filing the fact away to ask about another time, though. "Do you mind if I ask about her? Ásta?"

Smiling, I shake my head. "I don't mind. It's been a long time since she died. We lost her to one of the anomalies. Has anyone explained about the anomalies and what they did?"

"Yeah." He nods. "It must have been terrifying to live through. I'm so sorry for everything—everyone—you lost." He puts a hand on my thigh, right beside the notepad, and gives me a gentle squeeze. "I wasn't there, but I still know you did an amazing job leading your people through it."

The chuckle that escapes me is born of surprise, though that's quickly followed by gratitude. He might not have been there, but it's still nice to have someone reassure me that I didn't fuck everything up. "Thank you. For a while, I worried that none of us would survive, and I felt... guilty." I've never said this out loud to anyone before, and I hear the words as if from a distance. "I made the decision to close the dimensional portals during the species wars, and I made the decision to keep them closed afterward, when it was clear that humanity was still volatile and that visiting Earth could be risky. It's because the dimensional portals were banned that experimentation with temporal portals—"

"Okay, yeah, I'm going to stop you there," he interrupts, his tone gentle but very firm. "The person who made the decision to fuck around with time and then keep on doing it even after the consequences were discovered is the only person to blame for everything that happened after. Guilt is one of those messed-up emotions that doesn't always respond to logic, but you were absolved of any responsibility the second that asshat learned that tem-temporal portals were causing the anomalies and kept opening them anyway." He shakes his head. "Temporal portals. I never thought those were words I'd use in a sentence. Not unless it was about a sci-fi movie."

His words soothe the hurt I've been carrying for millennia, but I can't help smiling at his disbelief. "Stick with me, and I'll have you using words in all kinds of weird sentences." I hesitate. "If you wanted, I could teach you my native language."

"Your..." Jared's eyes widen. "Oh goddess, I never thought of that. Of course beings from another dimension wouldn't speak English! You even have an accent... But your English is so perfect."

"Thank you. We used a translator spell to help for the first few years, until English became second nature. But many of us still like to use our own language when we're alone."

"Translator spell," he mouths, then, "Of course you do. And I'd be so honored if you'd help me learn it. Add that to the list of things I want." He leans over to kiss my cheek. "But first, tell me about Ásta."

Sighing, I lean my head against his and think about my late wife. "We met here on Earth, actually," I say. "It was her first time visiting, but I'd been here at least half a dozen times before, and that time I'd come specifically to see some friends I'd made the last time. They suggested we go to another settlement for a festival, and Ásta was there with her sister and brother-in-law. The first time I saw her, she was casting spells to entertain some children —little tricks with moving lights and shadows, and her laugh caught my attention." I stop for a moment, lost in the memory of that moment. "By the time we both went home, we were firmly infatuated with each other. Back then, I was... well, there's not really an equivalent job here on Earth. A horticulturist, I suppose, but on an ecosystem level. My job called for me to travel a lot, and Ásta came with me. She was an archivist, so it fit well with her work. Has anyone mentioned the living archive to you?"

"No," he murmurs, and with my ear so close to his mouth, the sound seems to vibrate through me.

"It's something the elves and dragons developed—a kind of sentient memory. When any member of our species dies, their memories automatically upload to the living archive. Archivists have access to the memories of every elf and dragon who ever lived."

His breath hitches. "That's *amazing*."

"We think so. Ásta was so young to have been made an archivist, and we were all so proud of her. When I was invested, our lives changed a lot, but she saw it all as a challenge—a new perspective she could bring to her work."

"She sounds pretty great. I wish I could have met her."

I lift my head to meet his gaze. "She would have liked you. She always said that if she hadn't become an archivist, she would have been a teacher. She thought giving children foundational knowledge and a love of learning was the most important thing we could do for them—other than loving them."

The question is in his eyes even as he hesitates to ask it. "You two never had any kids?"

I shake my head. "No. We wanted to—planned to. But when you can choose how long to live, you always think you have more time. At first we were adventuring, and then after I was invested, we decided to wait until the life force released me from leadership." I shrug. "The anomalies ended that plan."

"I'm so sorry."

Mustering a smile, I lay my hand over his where it rests on my leg. "We would still have been waiting. Ásta devoted a great deal of time to working with children before we lost her, and I don't think she regretted that."

He turns his hand and laces his fingers through mine. "Is that something you still want? Children?"

It seems to be the night for me to be caught unprepared for questions. "I... Not right now. My situation hasn't changed—I would want to give my children more time and attention than I can spare while I'm king. It wouldn't be fair for them if the first thing they learned was duty—and it wouldn't be fair to my people if I let myself be distracted from said duty." The words hang between us. "That's not to say I think having a family would be—"

"I know what you meant," he says with a huff of laughter. "Kids need more attention than a partner does—a different kind of attention. They're dependent on their parents for everything. So... not right now for kids, but maybe in the future?"

"If that's something you'd want. It would need to be a mutual decision." I'm suddenly conscious that we never talked about this before.

"Hmm. If you'd asked me last month, I would have said no. I'm in my forties, and I work with children every day. But now that my future looks so different—longer, for one —I'm open to considering it."

I pick up the pen with my free hand and write that down on the notepad—along with teaching him Elvish. "Potential children to be discussed in the future," I say out loud.

"Perfect. That does bring me to another question."

"You can ask me anything."

"What, if anything, would you need from me to support your work?"

CHAPTER TWENTY-SIX

Jared

I watch Raðulfr's face closely as he considers my question. It's something I've been thinking about for the past week, but I'm not as nervous as I expected to be now that I've asked it. Our talk so far has been good—really good. We seem to be on the same page, and I'm more convinced than ever that this was the right decision for me to make. Raðulfr and I, even though we had a little hiccup, do belong together. I'm confident of that.

We just need to work out the details. A relationship with a nineteen-thousand-year-old elf king isn't something I've ever done before. There are bound to be some things I hadn't thought of.

"It's completely up to you how involved you'd like to be," Raðulfr says slowly. "If you'd prefer to stay out of it entirely, that's fine. We don't even need to publicly announce our relationship, if you like. Though the news would probably get out anyway." He grimaces slightly. "I have a range of after-hours functions and events to attend, and visits to elven settlements in other countries, so those nights and weekends I wouldn't be available to spend with you."

That makes sense—he's a head of state. "I don't want to keep us a secret," I declare, making sure to sound firm. We've had enough secrecy. "And I don't mind coming with you to some functions, where you think my presence would be helpful. But I don't want to give up my job, so I'd rather opt out of anything that might need me to take big chunks of time off work. I guess that counts as a limitation."

The way his face lights up makes me happy deep inside. "I wouldn't expect you to give up work," he assures me. "I know you love teaching. My engagement schedule is usually set a couple of months in advance, so what if I make sure that gets shared with you, and we can discuss which events you'd like to come to?"

"Yes." I nod, relieved. "That sounds good. I have more free time in the summer, so I could probably join you more often then," I suggest tentatively, and he grins.

"Perfect. We'll figure out what works best for us. We just need to stick to the only-honesty rule and make sure we talk about things."

The rush of happiness that overtakes me is almost dizzying. "Agreed. Is... Is there likely to be anyone who'll disapprove of us being together?" That's another thing that's been nagging at me—I don't follow celebrity gossip, but that doesn't mean I'm not aware that when celebrities date regular people, said regular people often get ripped apart by fans. Raðulfr isn't a celebrity, exactly, but he still has a lot of eyes on him and probably a lot of people who feel entitled to weigh in on his boyfriend.

"Possibly." His reply is candid and accompanied by an unhappy shrug. "Some people disapprove of everything, and politics is a tough game. But ultimately, none of those people have any influence on my personal life. The life force selected me to be king, and only the life force can remove me from that position—and it's been pushing me in your direction since we met."

My jaw drops. "It has?"

"Yes." His smile turns smug. "At first I was just grateful that it didn't disapprove, but in retrospect, it was actively encouraging every decision I made to be with you. Including that damn hockey game, so there's a good chance it wanted you to discover the truth sooner than you would have otherwise. Which is something I need to think about some more."

I rub my chin, still marveling that the essence that makes up existence wanted me and Raðulfr to hook up. "Do your people have fated mates?" I ask abruptly. It's a surreal concept, but then, so were elves and shifters just a few weeks ago.

Raðulfr pauses. "Not in the sense you mean," he says finally, and I'm a little surprised by how much that disappoints me. "A thing like one true mate for each person is too important to leave to chance—especially since we live so many lifetimes. The closest equivalent that I know of is paired souls."

That sounds a lot like soulmates to me. "Paired souls?"

"Yes. People whose souls will have a similar pattern of growth. They aren't fated to be together—an individual's soul could pair with those of several people. But unlike many other relationships, the people involved won't ever grow apart."

I think about that. "So they'll want to be together forever?"

"Not necessarily, but usually yes. There have been cases

when paired souls decided they wanted to separate, but it's rarely acrimonious. Mostly they both reached a place in their lives where they wanted to be single again."

I'm not sure I really understand. "Okay, so if they want to be together, they'll be soulmates, and later in life their paths won't diverge?"

He beams. "Exactly."

"So what's the difference between paired souls and fated mates?"

"Free will."

Huh. That actually sounds cool. "I can tell I'm going to end up with a lot of questions about your culture."

Raðulfr gives my hand another little squeeze. "I've already said I'll answer anything you want to ask. Hit me with them."

"I'll make a list," I promise, because my brain has gone predictably blank. "Um... what you said about a translator spell... I mean, I'm not doubting you, but that just seems so different from what I expected to be able to do with magic. Is that something I could learn, or does it come from the elf part of your ability?" It's mostly a rhetorical question. The way elves and even sorcerers do their thing is hard for me to get my head around. I'm not capable of ever doing what they do—it's like, I don't know... breathing underwater. Though less deadly. It's just not something my body and mind are able to do. A sorcerer can explain to me for hours how they weave power, but it's always going to be purely academic, because I can't even watch them demonstrate—only see the outcome. It was a disappointment when I realized that might mean that some of the things they do aren't going to be possible for me. I've been meaning to call Noah and ask about it, since he's the only human who might actually know, but I haven't got to it yet.

"Of course you could learn that," Raðulfr says, surprising—and delighting—me.

"Really?"

He must hear my excitement, because he chuckles. "Yes, really. The type of spellcraft you and I do is very similar—the main difference is how we power it. There might be some elements you'd need to handle differently from how I do it, but overall, it shouldn't be an issue once you learn how."

Huh. I guess I made some assumptions... "But it's not elemental. I mean," I add when his expression shifts to confused, "the stuff I've been learning in the program is all based around the elements. Air, fire... you know. I just thought..." I trail off as the confusion clears up.

"Ah. No, that doesn't have anything to do with capacity, but rather, security. Stringent guidelines were put in place for *who* could be invited to the program, but also what they could be taught. The knowledge you already have could potentially be extrapolated into a weapon of some kind, but that's a risk we had to take. Teaching it on such a small scale—candles and water droplets—was the compromise to hopefully prevent anyone from realizing what they could be capable of if they decided to turn supervillain." He makes an exaggerated face, even as I wonder about his choice of words—a risk they had to take? That makes it sound like the community didn't have a choice about teaching humans magic again.

Maybe he just means that it was unfair to expect community members with human spouses to let them die after a human lifespan.

"So the program was designed for humans to learn

limited magic? But I *can* learn to do more advanced things?" I don't understand the logic behind that, but I'm not the one running a government. There are probably political reasons for the decision that I'm not privy to. I'm fully aware that our agreement not to keep secrets from each other doesn't include classified government information—there's always going to be things Raðulfr can't talk about.

"That's right. I can help you work out how to adjust some elven spells, or Noah can teach you some things—or both. Both is probably the best option."

I nod slowly, already thinking about how much fun this is going to be—and how great it is that I'll have a much longer life to explore it all.

"I love watching you think about things that make you happy," Raðulfr announces, his eyes on my face and an indulgent smile quirking his lips. Just the sight of it makes up my mind that we've talked enough for one night.

"How do you feel about doing things to me that make me happy?" I give him my best bedroom eyes, and he straightens up immediately.

"Are you sure? I'm happy to take things slow—"

"Nope." Screw that idea. "You've proved that you're willing to answer my questions, and we've been apart way too long. I want to know what this couch feels like against my bare ass."

He makes a sound that goes straight to my dick. "Yes. That sounds... I want to know what your bare ass feels like everywhere."

"Great." I start to take off my sweater, but he catches my hand with a pained look.

"There's one thing you need to know first."

Uh-oh. I search his expression. "Is it bad?" He doesn't look like it's good.

"No. Yes. No. Maybe." He grimaces. "The anatomical differences between humans and elves aren't limited to..." He gestures to his face.

It takes a second for me to realize what he means, and then my gaze drops to his lap. "You mean you were using a glamor on your dick too?" I blurt the question out before I can think about diplomatic phrasing.

"Yes."

I swallow. "What are we talking here? Like... tentacles?"

To my relief, he laughs. "No, not tentacles. I can show you?"

My nod is automatic, and as he stands and his hands drop to his belt, a frisson of excitement races through me. It's a little surprising, considering I don't know what he's about to reveal.

His zipper goes down slower than I'd like, and then his pants and briefs drop to the floor. I barely notice as he kicks them aside, my attention fixed on his cock. It twitches under my gaze, then begins to harden, making the differences between our anatomy even more obvious.

Ridges. There are *ridges* running up the length of his dick, like rippling waves or perfectly even sand dunes or the corrugated cardboard sometimes used for art projects. They're visible even from two feet away, and I lift my hand toward him, stopping only briefly to glance up at Raðulfr's face for permission. There's a faint smile on his face that encourages me to continue, and I wrap my fingers around him.

Yep. Definitely ridges. They're firm under my grip, just the way he would be without them. I slide my hand up and down, wanting to see if they move at all, and Raðulfr's breath catches. The ridges stay solidly in place.

They would feel incredible inside me.

I swallow hard. I've used anal beads before and always loved the sensation. This would be even better—thick, warm flesh attached to the man I... well, it's pretty evident that I love him. I'd hardly be going through all this if I didn't.

"I love you."

An incredulous laugh escapes him. "Are you talking to me or my—"

"You! Goddess, I'm sorry. This must seem so weird, me saying that while I'm—" I let go of his cock hurriedly and stand up. He makes a disappointed noise, but this needs to be said without me groping him. "I swear it wasn't your dick that made me say it. Not exactly, anyway. I was thinking how it would feel better than anal beads"—my face is getting hotter with every word—"because it's attached to you, and I love you. Then I realized I've never said that to you, and it just... came out of my mouth." I wince. "I'm usually better at picking appropriate times and situations to make announcements. It's just been a confusing month."

"Every time and situation is appropriate if you're telling me you love me." He takes both my hands in his and lifts them to his mouth, kissing them one at a time. "I love you, too. I wanted to tell you before, but it already felt so dishonest to be sleeping with you without telling you everything." A shadow crosses his face. "I wish—"

"Stop. We've put that behind us, remember? I love you. You love me. I know all the big things now, and we're going to be happy together." Giddiness has taken over my whole body. We're in love!

CHAPTER TWENTY-SEVEN
Raðulfr

HEARING Jared say he loves me and that we have a happy future ahead of us is all my heart needs. I crash my mouth down on his and revel in the taste and feel of him, finally in my arms again.

Minutes—hours—eons might be passing, but all I care about is his lips against mine, his breath brushing my skin, his hands on my body and mine on—

His clothes.

Breaking the kiss but not pulling away, I murmur, "Take them off."

"Mmm. That would mean letting you go," he whispers, pressing a kiss to each corner of my mouth. "Don't stop kissing me."

That's an invitation I'm happy to accept, though I do whine a little when his arms disappear from around me—until one of his hands brushes against my stomach.

What's he—

The sound of jeans hitting the floor clues me in, and my chuckle is muffled by our kiss. He pulls back just enough to look me in the eye, a mischievous glint in his. "Are you laughing at my ingenuity?"

"I love your ingenuity," I promise. "Does this mean we're not taking our shirts off?"

"Not this time. Physical contact must be maintained until we've both come our brains out. It's the law of make-up sex."

I'd laugh again, but I hate that there's a need for make-up sex.

"Hey," he says, kissing the hinge of my jaw. "No sad face. Occasional make-up sex is part of healthy relationships. Next time it happens, we'll make sure we're both naked before we start."

This time I do laugh. "I love you. So much."

His smile warms me from the inside out. "Same. I love every inch of you." The smile turns wry. "I didn't intend for that to be a penis joke."

"Too late," I tease. "Come on, then... what are you going to do with all the inches you love?"

In response, he puts his hands on my chest and pushes lightly, following me back down onto the couch. "Why, Your Majesty"—a jolt runs through me. I never thought that honorific could be sexy—"I'm going to ride them."

He straddles me, trapping both our cocks between us as he leans down to kiss me some more. "We might need to move. Do you have lube?"

My breath catches as he moves his focus to my ear, nibbling the lobe and then licking toward the point. "Fuck," I gasp. "Do it again."

"Sensitive?" He scrapes his teeth over the cartilage, and my shiver answers for me. "This is going to be fun. But... lube?"

I force my eyes to focus and hold out my hand, concentrating just enough to cast the spell.

"Is that *magic lube*?" he exclaims. "We're going to talk about this later."

"I'll teach you," I promise. "Let me prep you now."

He rises slightly to give me access, and the friction makes us both groan. Then while I work on getting him ready, making sure to touch him exactly how he likes it, he goes back to teasing my ear.

"Enough," he pants at last. "Or I'll come."

"That's the goal," I point out, but obediently slide my fingers free, loving the way he shudders as I do.

Jared takes control, changing position and slowly lowering himself onto my dick. It's an exercise in torment for us both, as each ridge catches against his rim before pushing through, and we're both breathing hard by the time he's taken all of me.

Then he rides me.

On the fifth upward slide, I know I can't hold out much longer. It's been too long since I had him. I wrap my hand around his cock and stroke in time with his movements, the residual lube and his precum making it easy.

By the tenth stroke, he's moaning, a continuous low sound that matches what I feel.

By the fifteenth, we're both tense and gasping.

On the eighteenth, his gaze roams over my face and then meets mine. "You're beautiful. Never hide from me again."

That's all it takes.

Later, lying beside me in my bed, he curls his body around mine. "I'm so happy."

I smile into the darkness and revel in my joy. This is it. We've paid our dues. Nothing can go wrong for us now.

Something's wrong with Jared. In the two weeks since we reconciled, it's become very clear that he's unhappy about something. Not our relationship—I was worried about that, but it seems like the only time he smiles is when I talk to him. I can't doubt the way his face lights up when we're together. It makes me so happy to be a bright point in his life.

But something is making him more and more introspective and withdrawn, and my heart aches to fix everything for him. I've asked him what's wrong a few times, and he always smiles and says, "Nothing." So whatever it is, he doesn't want to tell me about it... yet. All I can do is be supportive and patient, and hopefully when he's ready, he'll share. At least I can be confident it isn't anything about *us*. He'd never go back on our no-secrets agreement.

Maybe he's just been nervous about today? Spring break began at his school, so finally he's coming to the office to officially "meet" the security team and some others. We thought that would be a good way for him to get his feet wet as my consort, especially since he already knows everyone on the security team. They've all had shifts at the condo recently, and Jared's been spending as much of his free time with me as possible. Margie really likes sitting at the huge windows and queening it over the city below. She had a checkup at the vet this morning, which is why Jared didn't come to the office with me. He'll be here as soon as he's dropped her home after the appointment, but now I'm wishing we'd made other arrangements. If he's nervous or worried about meeting people, being on his own isn't going to make that easier.

Abruptly, I stand and walk out of my office. It's too late for me to change our plans, but I can be waiting for him right outside the elevator. That way, he won't have to so much as look at anyone on his own. I'll be right beside him to be his champion.

"Where are you going?"

I jump, so involved in my own thoughts that I didn't notice Brandt falling into step beside me.

"Nowhere. Reception."

His face immediately lights up with dragonish curiosity. There's not much worse than a curious dragon—except maybe a stubborn one. They don't stop until they find the answers they want.

"Really? I adore Dáithí, but talking to him doesn't usually put a fatuous smile on your face."

I sputter. "I was *not*... I don't smile 'fatuously'!" I'm the king of the elves, which means nothing I do is foolish or silly unless I want it to be.

"Not usually," he agrees. "But this time it was. Were you thinking about Jared? He's coming in today, isn't he? I can't wait to meet him."

Alarmed, I stop walking and catch his arm. "Give him space. He's dealing with a lot of new things right now and doesn't need to be overwhelmed."

Brandt narrows his eyes. "Are you saying I'm ove— Of course I am. I'm the wingleader of all dragons. My mere existence is overwhelming to others."

Uh-oh. Now I've done it.

"But I'm offended that you don't know I'm planning to tone down my overwhelming aura so that your boo is more comfortable."

I blink at him. "My what?"

"Your boo. Honestly, Raðulfr, you need to make an

effort to learn modern slang. How can you relate to young people on their level if you can't communicate with them?" He rolls his eyes.

"I'm about ninety-nine percent certain that if any 'young people' had heard you say that, they would have laughed at you." I hold up my hand to stop his indignant reply. "But thank you for what I think was a promise not to overwhelm Jared. He's never met a dragon before... that he knows about." It's entirely possible he *has*, but not that I've witnessed or heard about.

Brandt instantly forgets that I offended him. "I'm the best one for him to meet, then. Aside from Cecylia. If I'd thought of it, I would have asked Percy to bring her in today. It's hard to be intimidated when a dragonet is wrapping you around her baby claws."

I can't stop the grin that forms as I picture Jared cooing over Cecy. It would be impossible for him not to— she has a way about her. I also suspect that she might be using some of her magic to charm people. Dragons usually can't when they're that young, but Brandt's her father, and he's exceptionally strong, so it's not completely out of the question that she's already able to access some of her power. Unlike elves, dragon magic isn't based purely on spellcraft, so there isn't as much focus and deliberation needed to make things happen.

We reach reception, and to my surprise, Jared is already there. He's talking animatedly to Dáithí, who's come out from behind his desk, and there's a warm smile on his face that gives me pause. Dáithí's great, but if Jared had been worried about coming here, it doesn't seem likely that five minutes of chatter would have relaxed him this much. Was I wrong about the reason for his unhappiness?

Even as I think it, he glances up and sees me. The way

his smile widens has me crossing to him without hesitation and dropping a kiss on his beautiful mouth. "Hello."

"Hi. Dáithí was just telling me the latest office gossip."

"Who left the buttprint on the photocopier, and was it a prank or something more salacious?" Brandt asks. "I'm on team salacious. We need a good office sex story."

Jared tries to hold back a smile as I sigh. "We do *not* need an office sex story, and might I remind you *again* about appropriate—"

"Management behavior, blah blah," Brandt interrupts. "I didn't say we need to make people engage in sex at work, just that I'm here for the gossip if they do." He extends a hand to Jared. "Hi. You must be Jared. I'm Brandt, Raðulfr's oldest friend, and I'm very pleased to meet you."

Jared glances at me as he shakes hands. "You're the dragon... wingleader? Is that right? I'm sorry, I'm still learning all the terminology."

Brandt beams at him. "You got it right. Raðulfr says you haven't met any dragons before."

With an apologetic grimace, Jared says, "Not that I know of. I'm still useless at recognizing community members who have their glamor on, though, so I might have."

Waving that off, my oldest friend declares, "You'll have to come to Here Be Dragons. I'll invite some people, and you can meet my Percy and Cecy, and I bet someone would take you flying. You haven't lived until you've been flying with a dragon. Raðulfr will bring you."

Alarmed—how is this not being overwhelming?—I suggest, "Maybe when the weather warms up some more." Or next fall. Six months should give Jared time to get his feet under him.

"Percy's your partner, right? The former lucifer?" There's an adorable line of concentration between Jared's brows as he tries to remember what he's learned in the past month.

"Yep," Brandt confirms, delighted. "And Cecy is our daughter. She'll be three later this year. You work with children, don't you?"

"Not as young as that, but yes. I teach kindergarten. It's always a challenge, and very messy, but I love it."

"We should get you involved with our education system," Brandt suggests, and I wish there was a way for me to kick him without Jared noticing. It's a thought I had myself, but I was going to wait until Jared had more time to get used to us all before mentioning it. I didn't account for the boundless enthusiasm of dragons.

"You have a separate education system?" Jared glances at me again. "Raðulfr didn't mention that."

"CSG had one in place when we migrated, and they very kindly allowed us to join and expand it. It's now a shared organization," I explain, but before I can continue, Brandt hooks his arm through Jared's.

"We can talk about all that later," he announces. "Jared's here to meet people. We'll start with Raðulfr's security team, because they'll get snippy if we don't, but then I'll take you to where the fun is." They start walking toward the hallway, and I shoot an alarmed look at Dáithí as Brandt continues, "Elves are great, don't get me wrong —I love them. Dragons look the way we do because we thought elves were awesome. But they really like their rules, and sometimes that makes them boring. You met Eoin, right? He can be a real stick in the mud. We dragons consider it our duty to make the elves loosen up."

"This is a disaster," I whisper, just as Jared looks back over his shoulder and grins at me.

"I think your guy can handle Brandt," Dáithí says. "He gave me an idea for managing Eoin that was inspired."

For a second, I'm torn between hearing all about it and chasing after Brandt and Jared before—

"—hardly dangerous at all. We almost always catch people before they hit the ground."

"Tell me all about it later," I tell Dáithí, racing across reception. I've waited too long for Jared to let Brandt accidentally drop him from over a thousand feet up.

CHAPTER TWENTY-EIGHT

Jared

I THOUGHT COMING BACK to school after spring break would help me to sort through the mess in my head, but it's been four days and I'm still just as off-center as before. Raðulfr's worried about me—I know he is—but I can't quite bring myself to tell him what's wrong. I'm scared it'll seem like I regret learning about the community, or worse still, that I regret being with him. Nothing could be farther from the truth. I was already committed to him—completely and undeniably, joyously in love with him—but hanging out with my new friends and spending time with Raðulfr's people over break has cemented the feeling that this is where I'm supposed to be. Every moment of my life has been leading me to this: To being a member of the Community of Species; to using magic as an everyday extension of myself; to being Raðulfr's helpmate and partner; to loving him and being loved by him. I'm not sure yet whether the life force has more of a purpose in store for me, but for now, I know this is exactly what I was meant for.

I'm just struggling with the destruction of the truth I'd built for myself.

With a little sigh, I sink into the reading chair. I'm supposed to be tidying the story corner, but it won't hurt anything for me to take a minute. I've already finished with the rest of the classroom, and it's not like I've got urgent plans this afternoon. Raðulfr won't be finished with work until close to six. The hours between now and then stretch ahead of me with yawning emptiness, and that depresses me even more.

Since when have I been the kind of defeatist person who can't find a way to fill time? There are a dozen things I could do and enjoy, but lately it's like the loss of my faith has led to a loss of enjoyment in everything.

"Jared?"

Startled, I lift my head and look toward the door. Gretchen raced out ten minutes ago, wanting to make an earlier-than-usual Yoga class, and I thought I was alone.

"Hey, Kaelynn." I muster a smile and stand. "What's up?"

Frowning, she ventures into the room. "You okay? You look... sad." Worry clouds her expression. "Please don't tell me you're having more relationship problems. I thought you two made up!"

I try not to wince. As much as I'd tried, I hadn't been able to hide my feelings from my closest colleagues after the hockey night fiasco, so I'd told them that Raðulfr and I had had a fight and were on a break. It seemed like the best way to get them to give me space and also not ask about the boyfriend I'd been gushing over just the previous day.

Kaelynn took it hard. Like, *hard*. And then when I told

them that we'd worked things out, she was elated. If I hadn't been so preoccupied with my own issues, I might have thought it was creepy how invested she seems to be in my love life.

"We did. We're fine," I assure her. "I'm not sad."

For a second I think she's going to argue the point, but then she makes a little humming noise and says, "You can talk to me, you know. About everything. I'm sure you have a lot of people to explain things to you and answer questions, but if you need to talk to someone who's been your friend from before, I'm here."

I open my mouth to ask what she means, then snap it closed again when it hits me. Is she— "Uh... you mean... Are you...?" I fumble for words. If she's still talking about my relationship woes or some random other things, asking if she's a member of the community would be a very fucking stupid—and dangerous, and illegal—thing to do. On the other hand...

She glances over her shoulder toward the doorway and the empty hall beyond, then flashes me a grin. "Shifter. Of the felid kind, since I'm very clearly not insane enough to be a hellhound."

"You're fucking joking." I blurt it out without thinking, then follow up with, "I'm sorry, I just meant—"

Her laugh cuts me off, and I sag in relief that I haven't offended her. Still, I can't believe this! All this time I had a source I've known and trusted for years that I could have talked to!

"It's fine," she assures me. "I would have said something sooner—I *wanted* to—but I didn't know if you knew yet, and then when the thing at the hockey game happened, I figured if you and the king didn't work things out, you might feel awkward knowing you work with me. Even though I have no connection to him or anyone he knows. Basically, I was overthinking it, and in the end I decided it was better to just wait and see what happened and keep being your friend in the meantime." She pauses, clearly a little anxious. "I hope that's okay."

"It's totally okay," I assure her, touched that she cared enough to overthink things. "And yeah, I'm not sure how I would have reacted if you'd said something when I was—" Wait. "What do you mean, the thing at the hockey game? How do you know about that?"

She scrunches up her face in sympathy. "I'm so sorry, but news got around. Nobody knew who you were," she rushes to add, as though that's a huge reassurance, "only that you were a human with the king. But the people who'd been sitting around you at the game saw and heard the whole thing, and..." She shrugs. "You'd already told me and Gretch his name and described him, so I knew. I mean, there was a chance it was someone else, but let's face it, how many men are going to have that name and description?"

"Yeah," I agree, trying not to let this get to me. It's not a big deal. The people who would have heard this news would all be part of the community, and they'd understand why Raðulfr hadn't told me. Nobody's going to think bad things about either of us because of this—not unless they were the type of person who'd think badly of us regardless. "Um, wow. I can't pretend I'm not totally surprised by everything you've said since you came in here. But I'm glad, and I will *definitely* be taking advantage of our friendship."

Kaelynn grins. "Good. Just so you know, I won't be

taking advantage of your new connections. I'm here for you, and that's all."

A rush of... relief? runs through me. Everyone Raðulfr has introduced me to or that I've met as a result of our relationship has been amazing and supportive, and I do count some of them as actual friends now, even though it hasn't been that long. But it's so nice to have someone who was *my* friend first to talk to about the community. "I never thought you would."

WHEN I FINALLY LEAVE WORK, the boost I got from my chat with Kaelynn dissipates, leaving me flat and overwhelmed by my own brain yet again. I don't want to go home, but there's nowhere else I want to go right now either, which leads to me driving around pretty aimlessly until a reckless driver runs a red light and I have to slam my brakes on to avoid hitting them. The adrenaline that floods my system is more grounding than anything else has been lately, and once the idiot driver is gone and I'm safely through the intersection, I look for somewhere to pull over.

To my surprise, I find that I'm downtown, near the stadium where Raðulfr and I—and Eoin, and thousands of others—attended that ill-fated hockey game. Street parking around here is rarer than hens' teeth, but instead of heading elsewhere, I impulsively pull into the nearest parking garage.

Expensive impulse. It better be worth it.

I'm not sure what I'm expecting when I approach the stadium. There are people wandering around, but not that many. The doors are open, which I wasn't expecting, so I pull out my phone and check the schedule on the website.

Open practice for the Warhammers.

They use the stadium for that? Huh.

Instead of going in, I turn left and circle around the outside. I'm still not sure what I'm looking for, but a walk won't hurt me.

"...fuck that! If you can't accept *me*, then I'm out. You knew exactly who I was when we started this."

Startled by the yelling, I glance around. There's hardly anyone around this side—the doors here are locked, and based on the wall up ahead, I think I'm getting closer to the utility area and loading docks. Off to the left, the wall gives way to a gate, and just on the other side, a man is pacing angrily and shouting into his phone.

Until he's not, because he's thrown the phone onto the concrete at his feet. I'm close enough to see a chunk of the screen fly off in a different direction to the rest of the handset.

"What are you staring at?" he snarls, and I lift my gaze to his face.

"Sorry. I wasn't... I was just walking past." Poor guy. Whatever that call was about sounded personal. I'd be pissed if a stranger overheard details of my private business, too.

His eyes narrow, and I take a step back. He's not that big, but I get the feeling that wouldn't stop him from doing a lot of damage. "I know you," he says, and my next step freezes in shock.

"Uh... you do?"

He moves closer to the gate and looks around before meeting my gaze again. "You're the human who's dating the elf king."

Oh. "I didn't realize I had celebrity status" is all I can think to say.

He shrugs. "I wouldn't say celebrity, but there are a couple of photos of you and him going around. And everyone knows you accidentally found out about us at a hockey game."

Great.

"Is that why you're here?" he asks. "Scene of the crime, and all that?"

My shoulders slump. "I don't know why I'm here. Maybe. My whole life changed that night, and I'm not sorry, but... I don't know who I am anymore. Except the weird person who unloads his personal business on a stranger. Sorry."

He snorts. "Just saying, I've had worse things unloaded on me." I'm still processing what that might mean when he adds, "I'm Felix Ansas, by the way. So now I'm not a stranger."

I blink at him a few times, pieces coming together. "You play for the Warhammers." The only decent player they have, based on what I saw.

"Yeah. I'm supposed to be inside, gearing up for practice, but I had to take a call."

We both look at the smashed-up remains of his phone scattered across the ground.

"It didn't go well."

"Sorry," I say again, mostly because I don't know what else to say. "Life sucks sometimes."

"Fuck yeah." He sighs and leans his head against the gate. "But I gotta put it behind me, because we have this stupid open practice, and Coach gets shitty when I'm in a bad mood."

I don't think asking how his coach reacted to him

attacking one of his teammates during a game is going to help his mood, so instead I ask, "Do you have open practices a lot?"

"Nah. Our practice rink doesn't have any seating for spectators, and hiring time here costs a fucking fortune. We do one with a charity meet-and-greet tacked on during the season, and this one right before playoffs."

"The Warhammers made it into the playoffs?" I can't keep the incredulity out of my voice. "I mean—"

He waves me off. "Nah, we're a shit team. But there's only four teams in the league, so even the team that's dead last is in the playoffs." He smirks. "One year, that team actually won."

"No shit?" That's kind of awesome.

"Yeah. So I've got high hopes—or I would, if my teammates weren't so..." He trails off with a growl.

I make a sympathetic face. "Maybe you can inspire them," I suggest, and he gives me a look that suggests I'm an imbecile. "Okay, so maybe not. No offense, but the game I was at, I was supporting the Glaives."

He shrugs prosaically. "They're a better team. We're the local team, though, and I don't want to move, so..."

Someone yells his name from behind him, and we both look in that direction. A bulky guy is gesturing impatiently from a doorway into the bowels of the stadium. Felix flips him off, then turns back to me with a sigh.

"I gotta go."

"Good luck. I think I'll support the Warhammers during the playoffs," I say impulsively, "so maybe try to win in spite of your teammates."

He scoffs, walking backward from the gate. "That'll be a trick. Hey, you know how you said your whole life changed and you don't know who you are?"

I wince. "Yeah?"

"Maybe a good person to talk to about that would be someone whose world was destroyed and had to start over on a completely new planet."

My jaw drops, and he shrugs.

"Just a suggestion."

CHAPTER TWENTY-NINE
Raðulfr

JARED DIDN'T MENTION HAVING any special plans after work, so when Eoin parks the car in front of his house, I'm surprised to see him on his front stoop, still in his work clothes. His keys are in his hand, and he's turned to look at us... did he just get home?

"I really can't convince you to talk to him about it?" Eoin asks for the tenth time as I reach for the door handle.

"He won't agree," I warn, and he takes that as a sign of compliance, sagging a little in relief.

"Just ask. Please. I'm getting desperate." His voice cracks on the last word, and I pat his arm.

"This *will* work out," I assure him quietly. "Just give him time." I get out of the car before Eoin can say anything else. He and I can talk later, but since we still haven't worked out a way for my bodyguards to be comfortable while I'm here, Jared and I only have a few hours together before I need to head home.

I'm hoping that soon we'll be able to move in together.

I don't want to bring it up until whatever is bothering Jared is resolved, but hopefully soon.

As I walk up the path toward him, my lips curve into a smile. I can't help it. Seeing him makes everything in my world better.

He smiles back, and it's different from usual... hesitant, perhaps? Or nervous. I'd worry, but when I reach him and lean in for a kiss, he meets my mouth with the same eagerness as always.

"Are you just getting home?" I ask when we break apart and he turns to put the key in the door.

He nods, glancing over his shoulder. "Yeah. I got sidetracked after work. Do you think we could talk before dinner? It's not bad, but—"

I kiss the side of his neck, breathing in the familiar lemon scent. "Of course we can talk, even if it is bad. Whatever you need."

For just a few seconds, he leans back against me. "I love you so damn much." Then he straightens and pushes the door open, his foot automatically moving to catch Marge before she can sneak out. I bend and scoop her up.

"None of that, miss," I chide, my mind racing. Is Jared finally going to tell me what's been bothering him? Even as I go through the motions of closing the door, letting Margie race off to the kitchen, and taking off my shoes, I prepare myself for anything. No matter what he says, I'm going to be calm and supportive and do everything he wants from me. If that means I need to stand aside and watch him be unhappy while he tries to fix this himself, then I'll... try.

By the time Jared has changed out of his work clothes and meets me in the kitchen, where I've poured glasses of iced tea for us both, I'm ready to be the best, most supportive partner ever.

His smile is tired and doesn't quite reach his eyes as he slides into a chair and picks up one of the glasses. "Thank you. You spoil me."

"Hardly. Though if anyone deserved spoiling, it would be you."

He takes a sip so tiny, it convinces me that he's done it for distraction rather than thirst, then sets the glass down. "I'm just going to dive in. I..." He hesitates. "I feel stupid about this, to be honest."

"What would you say if one of your students said that?" I ask gently, and get a rueful chuckle.

"Fair point. Okay, so feelings aren't stupid. I know this. But I've been struggling with some of my feelings lately." His gaze meets mine. "You've probably noticed."

I choose my words carefully. "I've noticed that you're not entirely happy."

He nods. "Yeah. I'm not, which is st— Which annoys me, because I have so much in my life to be happy about. So much I *am* happy about." He stops again, but this time I don't speak. He'll tell me when he's ready.

The silence lingers, and when he finally speaks again, his voice is rough. "When I cut contact with my family, it was... hard. I didn't—don't—like the person I was then. It took a long time for me to find myself, and a big part of that was becoming Wiccan." He swallows hard. "Learning to view the world through that lens and connecting with nature, with the god and goddess, it... I learned a lot about myself. Things I *like* about myself. I became who I am now through that process, and it grounds—grounded me. Anytime it felt like the world was out of my control or the ugly parts inside me might try to take over, I could perform a ritual and reconnect to my faith."

My heart aches for him. It's easy to see where this is going, but I don't interrupt. He's been carrying this for a while, and verbalizing it will give him more control of his feelings.

"But now..." He makes a shaky little sound that could be a sigh or a laugh. "I don't regret anything that's happened in the last few months. I'm so glad to know about the community, and so very, very happy that I have you. But now that I know the truth of the world, that the god and goddess don't exist and that I've been fooling myself with just another made-up religion... I feel adrift. I've lost my tether and I don't know who I am anymore." He gets quieter and quieter, until the last word is barely a whisper.

I wait, but it seems that he's done.

"Thank you for sharing this with me." I lay my hand on the tabletop, not far from his, leaving the decision of whether he wants to be touched right now up to him. It doesn't surprise me when he immediately reaches out and twines our fingers together. "In all the times we've discussed Wicca, I don't recall if I ever asked if the god and goddess were based on people."

He looks up, blinking. "I... sorry?"

"I know that some religions are based around people who lived in the past and were thought to have skills and powers. Christianity began because a sorcerer thought he could influence humans to behave with peace and kind-ness. Are your god and goddess—"

"Oh. No. There are some ties to the ancient pantheons, but nothing like what you're thinking."

"Then why can't they exist? You use magic every day.

You've felt it, shaped it—and you've touched the essence of life and nature. Aren't your god and goddess names for that? An easier form to relate to than amorphous energy?"

I can see him digesting that, the speed of his thoughts showing in his eyes. "You mean like... a different name for the life force?"

"Yes, basically. We elves call it the life force—the dragons do also, because they adopted our language. Our species connect very deeply with nature, and our relationship with the life force reflects that. Here on Earth, it's called the magic, and the native species have a slightly different connection to it. It's like flora and fauna—both are of nature, but yet not the same. They have the same source, but they're *not* the same." I give a little snort. "Dragons aren't even people the same way the rest of us are—they began as beings of pure energy, essentially electrical impulses. Then they saw us elves and thought it might be interesting to have a corporeal body."

Jared's mouth drops open. "Really? Is that why—Never mind. We can talk about that later. So... do you really think it's possible that the god and goddess are just a human name for the life force?" There's a tiny kernel of hope in his voice.

"Why not? Think about everything you've told me about Wicca. Your only rule is to do no harm. You don't proselytize or adhere to an arbitrary worship schedule. You don't have a hierarchy of priests who gatekeep access to your god and goddess. Your rituals are based around nature, the seasons, and the energy in the universe. You start no wars in the name of your deities, and you enforce no rules on others. I've lived a long time, Jared, and to my eyes, your religion is the way some humans have chosen to connect to the same essence of existence that the rest of us do."

For a few moments, we just sit and breathe while Jared thinks that through. At last, he makes a little *huh* sound. "I... I guess you're right. I never thought of it that way, but ultimately, my faith hasn't really changed. There's no back-story that's been disproved by what I've learned." He bites his lip. "The dualism of the god and goddess is the only true difference, but that's just a... categorization of energies."

"Exactly." I study his introspective expression, then venture, "I'm surprised this has been bothering you for so long. Haven't you felt that the energies were unchanged during your rituals?"

His breath catches, and he looks away. "I haven't done a ritual for a while. Since the night of the hockey game."

My heart aches for him. Jared's faith and his connection to the world through it have anchored him for well over a decade. No wonder he feels lost.

I stand. "Perhaps something small now?"

He nods, slowly coming to his feet. "Yeah. I think I could, now. Um... do you mind if it's just me? This time."

Since the first new moon ritual I watched, I've joined Jared in many more, but I understand that sometimes, some things need to be private. "Of course I don't mind. I'll get dinner started, and you take your time."

He leans in to kiss me. "You could watch, if you like, and then we can cook together after?"

For a dizzying moment, a vision rises in my mind's eye of the rest of my life, stretching year upon year into the future, filled with comfortable moments of togetherness just like he's suggesting. "That sounds perfect."

Jared goes to get his altar and things, and I scoop up Marge from where she's winding around my ankles, plaintively begging for her dinner. "Shush, you," I scold. "You're not that hungry—it's still early." The haughty "what would you know" look she gives me just makes me smile, and then she curls up against my chest for a nap, where she stays as I follow Jared outside and make myself comfortable on the bench.

The garden's changed since that first night I sat here, winter giving way to spring, and the new life coming into existence around us lends its own special energy to the space. One day soon, I'll show Jared how he can use his magic more directly with the plants he loves. Not today, though. We have time, and he needs something else right now.

The ritual he sets up in the circle is one I've seen before, a simple offering of thanks. His power hums as he closes the circle, and then he lays out the altar and lights his candles. They're green this time, and I'm fairly sure he's told me that represents growth, nature, and healing—though I could be mixing that up with another color.

Jared sits back on his heels before the altar, and his power rises again, his eyes drifting closed for a moment. He speaks no words for this ritual, though I'm certain he's thinking them. As the minutes tick past, the lines of stress fade from his face, and his aura becomes visibly lighter and less careworn.

He's found his peace again.

Breathing in the scents of the garden around me, with Jared's energy buzzing around me, Margie's warm, living weight in my arms and the knowledge that across the world, my people are finding their feet in their new lives, safe from the dangers that harried us for so long, I find my peace too.

And it's glorious.

EPILOGUE

Jared

SUMMER SOLSTICE

WHEN RAÐULFR MENTIONED that elves and dragons like to celebrate the solstice, I was thrilled that we would have this holiday in common. He joined me and some of my witch friends for Beltane, but it didn't hold any special meaning for him—except that it was important to me. So it was an exciting thought that we're both invested in the solstice.

This, though, is beyond my expectations.

I'm a solitary witch, but even when I've been with covens for celebrations, I've never experienced anything like this. Probably because all those witches were human and had no idea what kind of magic they could be capable of learning.

The dragons are hosting us, partly because they have this estate with lots of space and privacy, and partly because dragons love to throw a party. Steffen is the only one who doesn't look happy about it, and even he seems more mellow than the last time I saw him. Not that it would be hard to achieve that—every encounter I have with him makes me grateful that Eoin is Raðulfr's head of security, which is something I never thought I'd say.

Raðulfr and I have been here to visit the dragons before, at Brandt's insistence, but there weren't hundreds of people here then. It's amazing. Since the moment we arrived this morning, it's been a whirlwind of meeting new people, eating, saying hello to familiar faces, playing games with the children—the kind of games that include spell-craft and magic—and soaking in the joy of this stunning summer day.

And then, as the afternoon shifted toward evening, the rituals of gratitude began. For me, the solstice is a celebration of the sun and the energy and growth it brings to the world, but also of the change as the year begins to wane toward winter. The sun's cycle—the seasons—is inexorable, and we mark that with the solstices.

For the elves and, to a lesser but still large degree, the dragons, those things hold true, but today is also the time when they're most able to connect with nature. In winter, so many plants become dormant, but at midsummer, the world is alive and thriving. It's their holiday to give thanks for life and the eternal cycle of energy that sustains it.

I stand with the onlookers, awed, as children toss handfuls of seeds into the gardens and across the lawn, and then energy hums through the air as teens and younger adults coax the seeds to life. At first, there's nothing to see as roots are established, but then tiny shoots begin to unfurl, and those of us watching begin to cheer. From shoots to seedlings to healthy plants and saplings they grow, and joy eddies inside me. Raðulfr's confident that I'll be able to sustain my garden through the coming winter, and I can't wait.

The annuals that were seeded burst into flower, marking the end of this particular ritual, and we all applaud the flushed and happy young people who took part. I met nearly all of them earlier, and more than one confided shyly that it was their first time and they were nervous. Seeing their smiles now, I nudge Raðulfr with my elbow.

"Go tell them what a great job they did."

Chuckling, he loops his arm through mine. "I love how you care about their feelings. Come with me."

Glowing—on the inside—from his praise, even though that wasn't my motivation, I let him tug me along with him to where the teens are clustered together, excitedly recounting the details of their endeavor. One of them notices us coming and tells the rest, and then they're turning toward us with bright smiles and expectant gazes. Nobody is glamoured today, their heritage proudly on display.

"Well done!" Raðulfr proclaims. "That was beautiful work, all of you."

The smiles turn to wide grins and a chorus of thank-yous.

"We're proud to be here, Your Majesty," one girl says— Isla, if I'm remembering right. "Will you take one of the saplings?"

That's another tradition that thrills my green thumb. The flowering annuals will stay where they are, a gift to the host, but the saplings and young shrubs will be taken by the guests and transplanted in their own gardens. This ritual is from a time when the winters were particularly long and hard and summers not that warm. The elves in the affected region came together on the solstice to boost the growth of their faltering crops in the hopes of getting a decent harvest. Later, when the climate stabilized, they decided they were unwilling to give up something that had brought them so much joy, and switched from crops to trees and the like—a gift of thanks to nature for allowing them those bountiful harvests when they were so needed. They grow the trees to a point where they're strong enough to survive through winter, but still young enough to be transplanted with ease. Even now, people with shovels, plastic pots, and hessian bags are digging up the new saplings.

"We will," Raðulfr assures her. "I've already promised Jared."

The teens turn their attention to me, and one asks, "What did you think of the ritual, Consort Jared?"

I'm still surprised every time someone calls me that, but I no longer show it. Progress. The official title for Raðulfr's partner took some getting used to, though. "It was wonderful," I answer honestly. "I'm in awe of you all. Raðulfr is going to show me how it's done so I can look after my garden better, and I only hope I manage half as well as you did."

They fall over themselves telling me that I'll be fine, pleased by my words and eager to reassure me. It's sweet, and I'm not the only one who thinks so. There's a group of parents hovering nearby looking proud as punch and smiling indulgently.

We chat with the teens for a few minutes more before Raðulfr excuses us and draws me toward a cluster of people I recognize. Nearly all of them work at the DEA.

"How are you enjoying the day?" Ari asks me. He's one of my favorite members of Raðulfr's security team.

"Loving it. I've never been to a solstice celebration that

began so early, but I can see why you do. This is incredible."

"We'll light the bonfires soon," Dáithí says. He's standing beside Eoin, and they came together, but like always, there's a tiny bit of distance between them—the emotional kind. I know why, but despite all my hints, neither of them seems willing to take a risk in closing it. "The littlest ones will go inside for a slumber party, and the rest of us will keep going until sunrise."

That part of a solstice party is more familiar to me. Not all witches stay up the whole night—a small observance is really all that's needed, if they're so inclined—but usually when a bunch of us gather for a midsummer celebration, we bridge the sun's energy from dusk to dawn.

Across the circle, Cecy extends her arms and leans toward me. "Jawed!" she demands, and Caolan, the elf holding her, chuckles and moves forward to hand her over. Cecylia took a liking to me the first time I met her, when I spent half an hour playing hide-and-seek with her, and I can't say I'm mad about it. Though I got the shock of my life that day when I was holding her and she shifted into a tiny dragon.

Once she's perched securely on my hip, she points to the flower tucked behind her ear and says, "Pwetty." It's more a demand than observation.

"It's a beautiful flower," I agree solemnly. "Almost as beautiful as you." That gets me a big grin and a wet kiss on the cheek, before her attention is caught by a group of kids running past.

"Down!" She squirms until I obey, then runs off after the kids. I take a step to follow, but Caolan catches my arm.

"She's fine," he assures me, nodding toward the dragon

supervising the kids, who waves back. "The parents of the littlest ones set up rotating shifts to watch them today. In any case, Steffen's got so many cameras around the grounds that it wouldn't take long to track down anyone who wandered off, and the whole place is warded against anyone with ill intent. This is the safest place in the world for them to run around and test boundaries."

"That must be paradise for them," I muse. A lot of little kids are risk takers anyway, not having learned to be afraid, but most of them don't have dozens of acres of woods and gardens to run wild in... or rudimentary magic, or wings.

"It really is," Caolan confirms. "For their parents, too."

Shit. That was so insensitive of me, when not that long ago these people were living inside a forcefield and expecting to die. I'm grateful the rest of the group has moved on with the conversation and didn't hear my faux pas. "I'm so sorry, I—"

He waves off the apology. "I knew what you meant. It's a miracle for us all to be able to watch them be so free and fearless." He drags his gaze away from them and smiles at me. "I'm glad we're getting the chance to talk. Alistair said you turned down his invitation to join the brohood."

I glance over my shoulder, in case Alistair's behind me. He's here somewhere—he has enough friends among the dragons and elves that he's always on the guest list. "I'm still trying to find my feet with everything," I explain. "I'm grateful for the friendship, but I'm not sure I have the bandwidth right now to be a full-fledged bro." Not to mention, I'm not sure it would set the best example for the consort to get involved in some of the things I've heard they've done in the past. It was tempting, though. They're all a lot of fun.

Caolan nods understandingly. "I get it. Brohood is a big commitment. The invitation stands if you change your mind, but that's not what I wanted to talk to you about."

It's not? Then why did he bring it up? "Oh?"

He gestures behind me, toward Raðulfr. "You and the king are solid, right?"

Like always, I have to hide my amusement at hearing modern slang come from a man who looks like he could have stepped off the set of *Aliens: Lord of the Rings*, which, if anyone ever made it, would be an epic movie that I'd watch the heck out of. "We're solid," I confirm. "I know it's only been a few months and that we had a rough start, but you don't need to worry about—"

He shakes his head, silvery blond hair sliding over his shoulders. "I'm not worried. I'm just... trying to decide if I should tell you something."

Pushing aside my instinctive fear reaction, I study his face. It's serious, but not in a bad way. Not like he has bad news; more like he knows something that's important. "Would it make me happy or sad?"

"Not sad," he says immediately. "I think it would make you happy, but I really don't know you that well yet."

A heavy, familiar arm comes around my waist, and I lean back into Raðulfr as he asks, "What would make Jared happy?"

"We're not sure if it would," I caution him. "Caolan's trying to decide if he should tell me."

"How intriguing. What—" His body freezes, going solid against me, and I straighten and turn to look at him. He's staring at Caolan.

I look at Caolan too.

"Your Majesty, if you ever wanted to ask me something, I would answer," he says.

The penny drops. Since that first time Raðulfr and I talked about the elves' version of soulmates—paired souls —it's come up another time. Two of his people came to him to ask if he could see whether they were paired. That blew me away. I'd thought it was just a "feelings" thing, but apparently, there are elves who can actually see when others have compatible souls. Raðulfr is one, and he mentioned a few others who could also.

Including Caolan.

"It wouldn't make me sad?" I demand, and the tall elf shakes his head again. "I'm asking, then. Are Raðulfr and I paired souls?"

I swear Raðulfr is holding his breath.

Caolan smiles. "Yes."

The King of the Elves buries his face against the side of my neck, and I wrap my arms around him, mouthing "Thank you" to Caolan as he winks and slips away.

"It wouldn't matter," Raðulfr mutters, his voice muffled against my skin. "Even if we weren't, it wouldn't matter to me."

I kiss his hair. "I know. Nor me. But now we know our souls are on the same growth path. That's free will and fate, both giving us eternity together."

He lifts his head, and his eyes are wet. "Free will and fate." And he kisses me under the solstice sun.

Thanks for reading *Wooing the Wiccan*! Raðulfr's story has been a long time coming, and he's earned his happily ever after. Next up is Eoin and Dáithí's story, *Enticing the Elf*.

If this is your first introduction to the Community of

Species world, welcome! The best place to start is with Sam and Gideon in *Demons Do It Better*.

We talk spoilers in my Facebook reader group,
RoMMance with Becca & Louisa.
Or you can subscribe to my newsletter to get all updates and access to bonus scenes: https://bit.ly/LouisaMBonus.

For early access to chapters of my upcoming books, artwork, and other bonus material, check out my Patreon here: patreon.com/louisamasters

ALSO BY LOUISA MASTERS

Saddles & Suits

Alistair's Extraordinaries

Grave Situation

Elemental Men: The Complete Series

Style Me

Rebrand

Couture

Elf Magic

Wooing the Wiccan

Enticing the Elf

The Collective

Higher Demon

Demon Hunter

Demons-In-Law

Asher

Micah

Zachary

Franklin U

Mr. Romance

The Holigay Hookup *related novella

Batting Style

Ghostly Guardians

Spirited Situation

Vortex Conundrum

Conduit Crisis

Gateway Catastrophe

Here Be Dragons

Dragon Ever After

The Professor's Dragon

The Dragon Experiment

Conspiracy of Dragons

Hidden Species

Demons Do It Better

One Bite With A Vampire

Hijinks With A Hellhound

Sorcerers Always Satisfy

Hidden Species Box Set

Met His Match

Charming Him

Offside Rules

A Christmas Chance (novella)

Between the Covers (M/F)

Joy Universe

I've Got This

Follow My Lead

In Your Hands

<u>Take Us There</u>

Novellas

Fake It 'Til You Make It (permafree)

One Golden Night

O Hell, All Ye Shoppers

Out of the Office

After the Blaze

Blokes Down Under Novella Collection

ABOUT THE AUTHOR

Louisa Masters started reading romance much earlier than her mother thought she should. As an adult, she feeds her addiction in every spare second. She spent years trying to build a "sensible" career, working in bookstores, recruitment, resource management, administration, and as a travel agent before finally conceding defeat and devoting herself to the world of romance novels.

Louisa has a long list of places first discovered in books that she wants to visit, and every so often she overcomes her loathing of jet lag and takes a trip that charges her imagination. She lives in Melbourne, Australia, where she whines about the weather for most of the year while secretly admitting she'll probably never move.

http://www.louisamasters.com

www.ingramcontent.com/pod-product-compliance
Lightning Source LLC
Chambersburg PA
CBHW032001050726
47590CB00006B/2004

9781923035461